Lithuanian Short Stories

Edited and Translated by
Tadas Klimas

Lithuanian Short Stories

Dedication: To St. George's RC Parish, Rochester, New York.

———◆———

Lithuanian Short Stories
ISBN-13: 978-0-9818441-1-4
ISBN-10: 0-9818441-1-1
Published by: Transnational Academic Press
http://transnat.uuuq.com/

ACKNOWLEDGEMENT

I am grateful to my father, Antanas Klimas (Professor Emeritus, University of Rochester), for encouraging the translation of these short stories and other writings and for publishing them in the editions of the journal *Lituanus* which he edited.

Table of Contents

FOREWARD

I translated all of the short stories and other writings in this book over the years in the traditional manner of Americans of Lithuanian descent — on the weekends and evenings, unrecompensed, as a labor of ... well, it was either love or something, I am not sure what. Protest? Principle? Back then, Lithuania was occupied by the Soviet Union, and I suppose the effort of translating these stories was in keeping with an idea common to the 'Lithuanian diaspora community' that to 'contribute' to Lithuanian culture in some way was to help bring about the restoration of Lithuania's independence and thus to restore justice. Quite radical, quite mad.

But Lithuania did re-establish its independence, and therefore I suppose our common efforts were not wasted.

Eight of the translations herein are of short stories. All of their authors fled the Soviet occupation of Lithuania during World War II, with the exception of one, who moved to the West in the late Soviet era.

The other two pieces are not short stories. Both are remarkable pieces of prose, written during the period of the Sąjūdis movement in Lithuania which culminated in Lithuania's re-establishment of independence in 1990 (recognized by most Western powers in 1991). The authors of both of these pieces continue to reside in Lithuania. These two writings give one the feeling of the times, a most amazing time in which a forgotten country re-asserted itself.

Each story, indeed, each translation herein, has a short introduction, specially written for this volume. After each story there is a brief publishing history and a bio of the particular author.

What are these stories about? The collection includes the first Lithuanian story written in the fantasy genre and stories written during the prewar period and set in that time, which now seem like period pieces. Then there are two about the human predicament in a war-torn country under foreign occupation. Another is set in the early 1980s in the Great Lakes region of the United States, but it relates back to Lithuania and the question of its fate.

The tone of the stories varies enormously. Obviously, the fantasy story is rather mystic, and the ones about war-time experiences are sober and sobering, but then there are some of a lighter tone (*Romance on a Bus*), others of a barely-restrained pastoral sexuality (*Flax Blossoms*), and some which seem to defy description, for instance, *Barborytė*.

This is the third anthology of Lithuanian short stories available in any format and the first to be available also as an e-book.[1] In the preparation of this volume I have changed and edited the translations of all of these short stories and other writings, all of which, save the last story (*Barborytė*), had been published previously. They are not exactly like the original translations. In translating, I did

---

[1] There are only two other collections of Lithuanian short stories in English translation that I am aware of. The first was published in 1959 by Stepas Zobarskas and has been long out of print. The second was published in 1992. It was edited by Violeta Kelertas and it contains stories published in occupied Lithuania. This anthology is entitled *Come into My Time: Lithuania in Prose Fiction, 1970-90* and is still in print.

not hold to the idea that the translated version should read entirely as if it had been written in English by a native speaker. My goal in translating is to reproduce as well as possible the tone of the original, and sometimes I find it is better to have the prose be somewhat stilted, as that adds to the effect. Why should a piece written in Lithuanian in the 1930's sound as if it were written in colloquial early 21st century English?

The Lithuanian characters (with diacritical marks) can be pronounced as follows: š = sh; č = ch; ž = zh (like a Frenchman pronouncing 'zuzu the cat'); ū and ų = oo as in 'you' ; ą = ah ; ė like the French é; ę = like a long 'ehh'; į = ee.

All of the stories in this volume are very good. The finest, I think, is *The Cross*, by Jurgis Jankus. Ostensibly the story is set in a Lithuania of centuries ago, but it really could be taking place much of anywhere and, perhaps, anytime. See for yourself. It is the first story in the collection.

Tadas Klimas
March, 2009

THE CROSS

Jurgis Jankus

Translated by Tadas Klimas

There is something about this short story. It is compelling, and once read, it seems to stay with you, like a feeling associated with a good friend or a good deed.
This story was originally translated back in 1973 and published in an academic journal. Somehow, the editors of a magazine which at least back had a very wide distribution, Short Story International, got wind of it and republished it in the following year.
I'd thought it forgotten. But then in 2003 it, that is, my translation, was re-translated into Vietnamese and published in a Vietnamese Christian magazine out of Texas.
This short story is a masterpiece. It is the capstone of the collection, and it is a profound pleasure to be able to make it available to you.

If thirty years ago someone happened to walk down a small country road from Girkalnis to Šimkaičiai, he may still remember — near the edge of the village of Pakalniškiai, on the slope on the castle-hill where the road turned through wet meadows — there stood a cross, a singular cross, quite unlike other crosses scattered by the roads. The cross itself resembled other crosses: made of two thick, solid oak logs, darkened with age, rain-wearied, etched with little cracks from sun and cold; tufts of greenish and gray, pattern-making moss grew from them. The top of the cross and its arms ended with large, time-worn knobs. They were of another, less hardy wood, and appeared to have been added much later. Probably some craftsman had wanted to embellish, with his skill, that large, axe-hewn mass.

One might have passed the cross, itself, without noticing it, for similar if not so massive crosses dotted Lithuania's roadsides. But the figure of Christ arrested everyone's attention: one could hardly pass it without stopping or at least glancing back several times. The wooden Christ was so unusual, even today I can't understand why it never became world famous, unless God himself in his divine unpretentiousness wanted it not to be. The figure was fully life-sized and carved entirely from one single piece of wood. Even the arms had not been added. Its wind-wearied limbs quivered with exhaustion; its head tilted forward and to the side, rapt in thoughts about weariness, and pain... and perhaps even tomorrow's and the next day's worries. The head's usual crown of thorns was missing, and so was the roof-cover that usually protects the holiness from the penetrating rain and hail. Only someone had placed upon the downcast head a wreath of corn flowers, bluebells, buttercups, and other wild flowers. This might have been done even by a taller child, since the cross was so low; the figure's toes almost touched the ground. It seemed the bottom had rotted more than once, and had been replaced, shorter, each time. If so, it should be unusually old, because oak rots very slowly. Only why did time not erode from his face the breath of life? One stood looking and waiting for the downcast eyelids to suddenly open. And the eyes would look directly at you, the lips would open, and one would hear the words the world had long awaited; the words which theologians and poets have been searching for in thousands of volumes. But they would come to you, just as natural as the blossoming of a daisy.

"Are – are you praying, or just ... looking?"

The woman's voice startled me out of my reverie and even made me jump a little. I had been so engrossed in the cross that I had not noticed her as she shuffled up to me. A very old woman indeed, a little bent with age, with a greatly wrinkled face. But her eyes were alive and young. Time with its masterly fingers was unable to touch these eyes, just as it was unable to touch the face of Christ on this cross. In one hand she held a basket of beet-leaves and in the other some newly-pulled carrots.

"It's beautiful", said I, glancing at the Christ.

"Yes, beautiful — and precious! But it won't be here for long," sighed the old woman, wiping her brow with her hand.

"Why? The cross looks like it could still stand for a long time."

"It could, but it won't. Maybe a year or two. You see, the feet are nearly touching the ground. When they do, he'll take his cross and go elsewhere. Some morning we'll just wake up and he won't be here anymore."

I felt like arguing, but I had already learned not to contradict local beliefs directly. I kept silent for a minute, looking at Christ's face and especially at his lips, at times seeming to quiver as if they wanted to speak. Then I said:

"A wonderful, beautiful work. Who carved it? If he is still alive, I would like to meet such a masterful carver."

"No one, mister, could have carved this cross. The last Candlemas saw my ninety second. I've lived here all my life, and the cross hasn't changed a bit. Not by a hair. When I was just this tall," indicating with her hand some distance from the ground, "I already made garlands for him. Only then I couldn't put them on. I couldn't reach. Even grown men couldn't; they had to get something to stand on. And when I wanted to kiss his feet, I had to ask somebody to lift me up; but now the smallest child can easily reach it. Men's sinful eyes can't see... but it sinks and sinks..."

"Some sort of underground well is probably underneath", I started explaining, "Some men should get together and move it."

11

Inwardly I thought such a treasure should be in a museum under glass, but I didn't say so, afraid of offending and silencing her. Even my suggestion to move it made her shake her head.

"Nobody raised it, mister, and nobody'll move it!" she sharply pronounced.

"No one raised it!" I marveled.

"Of course not. He came of himself and chose his own place; only, we keep piling all sorts of troubles, worries, and evil deeds on his head. That's why he keeps sinking and sinking..."

She stopped talking. So did I. Both of us gazed at the cross. She settled herself slowly upon the thick green grass by the road. And I sat down beside her, thinking that whole cross should be brought to a museum. But I didn't say anything.

She took a piece of hair-grass and started winding it around her fingers like a ring. She wore no other rings. Maybe she had never gotten married or maybe she had taken off her ring, polished from wear, and put it into her hope chest to be buried with her.

"I know you young and educated people have trouble understanding things," she said after a little while, "you've got to have everything checked, re-checked, and written down first. Especially — written down in books. I've read books, too. And I still read, even now, thanks to the Lord. He gave me good eyes. And I read the papers, too. And while reading them, I keep thinking there is no way to get everything written into books?! Take our cross, for example. No one's going to put that into a book. Who can measure what burdens have been piled upon his shoulders and his heart!"

And she paused again. She had unwound the grass from her fingers and now was chewing on it. Suddenly she smiled.

"I still have almost all my teeth. God has really been good to me. I've had a fine life. Once in a while I say to myself, 'Mary, for such a life you should have made him many more crowns than you did! Of course, you've read in books of the terrible years of the plague," she abruptly turned the conversation from herself. "Now no one ever talks of them, but when I was young, they were still on everyone's lips. Though they hadn't lived through the plague, they remembered it from their parents and grandparents. They said, a kind of wind blew and everyone lied down — lied down and didn't get up again. Others told of dark horsemen that passed in the night; and that where they passed, half didn't rise in the morning, and the next morning — the other half didn't. Only those happening not to be home that night, or those praying beneath the cross remained untouched by that calamity; but, for that, they had to tend the sick and take care of the animals.

Our village was a lot larger in those days. They say it had rained the whole day, then, when it cleared in the west a bit, came flocks of black crows. They covered all the trees and roofs. Dogs whined at doors to get inside. Even men shivered at the crows' screeching. It got dark a lot earlier than usual. Next morning the crows had gone, but people began to fall like leaves. Only the Darvydas' Ignacas remained all right. He had gone, the day before, to press oil from hemp seeds.

Returning after daybreak, he found his household all struck down by the plague. All his neighbors, too. One or two still moved around that day, but by the third — he was left alone. They say he was a strong man. Nowadays his sort doesn't exist anymore — people have taken to an easy life. But they can afford it now. In those days, however, they had to work hard; and that's why they grew up like oaks. Neither rain, nor cold, nor trouble scared them. They didn't scare Ignacas. During the day he went from one farm to another. He looked after the animals and helped the sick, and carried the dead from the houses. Do you see, over there that mound near the middle of

13

the village? There in the sand he dug a hole and piled the dead like logs. Those he piled during the day he buried in the evening, so that the dogs wouldn't get them during the night.

One day after burying that day's dead he couldn't believe his eyes: through the meadows came a man carrying a huge cross. Ignacas, although tired and exhausted, went to meet him and offered to help him. Ignacas thought it's probably someone wanting to erect it over his dead. But although the man looked vaguely familiar, he was a total stranger. Ignacas offered to help carry the cross at least as far as his yard. He said: "I'll milk the cows, and give you something to eat, and then I'll hitch up the horses, or something. You can't drag that heavy thing anywhere by yourself." In his yard he leaned the cross against the house (grandmother used to show where the wall was scratched near the end of the house), and left the man to sit by the side of the house, running off to milk the cows. Later, while feeding him bread and milk he asked, "Where are you carrying that cross from?" "From far away. You might say, from the ends of the earth," smiled the stranger. "And always alone? Have so many died that no one can help you?" "No, just that everyone has other things to do." "I could help you," Ignacas offered sincerely, "but who would take care of the sick and bury the dead? And the animals have to be looked after, too. I mean, they can't be just let loose into the fields. If it isn't far, then I could carry it a bit, until nightfall. If it's far, then I'll hitch up the horses. You'll return them later. You just can't carry that weight by yourself". The man smiled again. "Not far now", he said, getting up from the bench and trying to take up the cross. He looked so weak and tired that Ignacas jumped up and cried: "Wait, I won't let you carry it alone. Take the end, and I'll take it by the arms!"

Ignacas took the cross, settled it upon his back and felt how his feet sank into the ground, how his shoulders bent as if he had placed the world upon them. But he clenched his teeth and strode, though trembling, though staggering. "Lord, help me," he quietly whispered. "Just not to fall, just not to kill myself.

Who's going to take care of things tomorrow?" They shambled down the street and went a ways out of the village. The stranger said, "That's enough. Leave me here." "So you're going to try carrying it yourself?" asked Ignacas over his shoulder. "Let's put it down here. I won't carry it farther. This will be a good place," smiled the man again. "If you wanted to raise it here, you should have said so. I would have brought a spade. We won't be able to put it up without one." "Don't worry. Go home now. You have to rest, too." "Then let's go together. If you won't take a bed, lots of straw is in the barn. I'll give you plenty of blankets." But the man sat down on the cross, leaned his chin upon his hand, and raised his eyes to Ignacas. "Thank you for your kindness," he said, "but I'll stay here. Does it matter, where God's man rests his head? And thank you also, for lightening my load. Go, at home the sick, the dead, and the animals wait for you, and I want to sit awhile and muse." Ignacas turned to go, then looked back at the man lost in reverie. "Listen," he finally said, "you should be from around here somewhere. I would almost swear I've seen you some place before." The man lifted his eyes up again, looked and smiled. "Maybe I'm not from far way, maybe from even nearer. But now it's getting really dark. Come tomorrow, we'll talk some more. I'll wait here."

Ignacas wanted to say something more. But he couldn't find the words. So he shrugged his shoulders and left. In a minute, he began to feel a deathly fatigue. It seemed every step threatened to be his last. "Probably the sickness is getting me now, too," he thought. "If I fall, there will be no one left to dig a grave for me." Thinking this he tottered home, fell upon a bench and woke only the next morning. He got up and was amazed. In his house all the people were well. The whole village was well again. The dead stayed dead, but those who hadn't died walked as if they had never been sick. They worked around their houses, looked after their animals, buried and mourned for the dead. But all rejoiced that the plague had left as suddenly as it had come. Ignacas ran and helped everyone, and showed them who had been buried where. Only around midday he remembered the strange man. If he still waited as he had said he would, he'd be hungry. Ignacas filled a pitcher with milk, took a large hunk of bread, climbing into the attic, cut off a slab of bacon, and hurried out. Just outside the village he stopped, startled. In front of him stood a huge cross, upright, and standing there upright it looked even larger than the one he'd carried the day before. Ignacas felt ashamed. Obviously, the man had waited and waited, until, finding a shovel, he had put up the cross himself, and left, for not a living soul was around. Looking at the fields in hope of seeing the stranger, Ignacas approached the cross, lifted his eyes and froze: from the cross gazed at him that same man he had left yesterday sitting and saying he'd much to ponder about. He let the pitcher of milk and the bread fall from his hands; he took off his cap and did not even notice his knees beginning to bend. "My Lord, Jesus Christ!" he whispered, "Yesterday you came to me, and ate, and drank, and we talked, and I didn't recognize you. Forgive me, Lord." "Rise," quietly and very naturally spoke Christ. "Now you recognize me, and that's good. Go and tell everyone what happened yesterday. Let all carry their joys, worries, troubles, sins, and repentance and put them on this cross. Good deeds will raise it, and evil ones will press it into the ground." Christ fell silent, and in Ignacas' sight changed into a wood-carved figure. For many years he stood tall, and sometimes it seemed he even started to grow. Then he began to sink. Now you can see for yourself how little is left; and we just keep piling weight on his head. No one told me, but I feel it in my old heart... just when his feet touch the ground, he'll take the cross upon his shoulders and go to find another place. We'll be orphans. Justly, but still orphans."

With these words the old woman rose, reached up to fix the flower wreath, knelt to kiss the nail-pierced feet, and went away.

As if entranced, for several minutes I looked at the few inches between the feet and the sheep-cropped grass, then suddenly a thought hit me — what if this was no myth, but the truth? What if he gets up, takes his cross and leaves, not to find another place, but leaves this earth? And what will happen, if leaving he takes with him the command to love one's neighbor that even after two thousand years remains so foreign to us?

I looked around. In the midday heat sank the fields, orchards, and the village houses. Not the smallest line in Christ's face moved — his eyes calm, gaze, intense upon eternity. No one was prepared to give another answer, except the one dolorously reverberating in my heart.

* * *

Jurgis Jankus was born in Lithuania in 1906. He already enjoyed an excellent reputation as a novelist in pre-war Lithuania when he had to flee his homeland to escape the Soviet occupation. Settling in Rochester, New York, he worked in factories and raised four boys with his wife, Kotryna. He wrote at night and on the weekends, and published a number of collections of short stories and two plays. In 1991 he traveled to Lithuania, which had newly re-established its independence, for the first time since WWII. There he greatly enjoyed the many literary events which were organized in his honor. Jurgis Jankus died in 2002 and is buried in Rochester, New York.

The title of this short story in the original Lithuanian is *Kryžius*. It appeared in a collection of Jurgis Jankus' short stories entitled *Užkandis* [The Snack] (Ateities Literatūros Fondas 1973).

This English translation was originally published in *Lituanus*, the Lithuanian Quarterly Journal of Arts and Sciences, Vol. 20, No. 3 (Fall, 1974). It was reprinted in *Short Story International*, No. 16 vol. 3 (1974).

A Vietnamese translation (from the English translation) was published in the Christian magazine *Dan Than* in 2003 (No. 11/12, Katy, Texas).

IN THE TIME OF THE HANGING
(DEMOCRACY IN THE SOVIET UNION)

Algimantas Čekuolis

Translated by Tadas Klimas

This short, incredible, piece is not a short story, but a commentary or opinion-piece. It is both exhortative and didactic. It was written during Lithuania's struggle to re-establish independence from Soviet occupation and hegemony. While of literary merit, it is in keeping with the tone of that struggle. Highly principled, intelligent, disciplined, and adamant.
At the time this writing was published, Lithuania's independence was not yet recognized by the Western democracies.

Democracy in the USSR, short-lived, having neither spread nor gathered strength, nor having penetrated deeper into many regions and areas, only kissed by some republics but not embraced, on 17 November of this year began to die. It was then that presidential rule *de facto* was initiated throughout the whole USSR. Let it call itself the government of the "Federation Council," but the members of that council are appointed by and completely controlled by the president. He will be able to try to repeal any laws at all, whether enacted in the Supreme Soviet of the Soviet Union or in the republics. He will be able to issue his own laws, appoint his own governor-generals, and so on. You saw, you heard. And you remember the past.

The Kremlin's deputies just applauded. Now we will have some order, the stores will be fully stocked, robbers will disappear from the streets, and railroad cars full of products won't be lost for half a year in the wastelands.

Will it be like this, can it be like this?

The hundred story tall Soviet skyscraper is built on a foundation of sand. Two of its supports — Russian imperialism and communist ideology — are disintegrating before the eyes of everyone. They can buttress the walls with any kind of ramparts, run to paint the facade, shriek like crazy so that no one would hear the edifice cracking — but it won't help. In the time of the hanging of Saddam Hussein, you can't bring back old Joe Stalin. Moreover, Old Joe had the prophetic power of a founder. He was able to say, wait, you'll see how wonderful the building will look. Mikhail has inherited that building, and everyone can see just what it is like. Joseph was still able to lie that he was not expanding the Russian empire, but was uniting nations in brotherhood. The bolshevik idea was still forceful, and there were people who would have gone to their deaths for (and even more that did go to their deaths because of) that idea. Now the tide of reality has washed the cement out of the foundation, and you can no longer just station a soldier with a gun behind the back of everyone. No one is able any more to put 20 million in jail or to shoot 10 million so that the rest would be afraid. There will be no skyscraper.

I spent that long weekend in the Kremlin. A few of us participated as observers; as befitted those who, once elected by the people of Lithuania, had existed after 12 March. I spent most of my time in the anteroom, watching everything on television monitors and sharing my thoughts with foreign journalists and television crews.

How hotly, emotionally, and profoundly spoke the deputies! "We must take measures, we must quickly take measures, we must very quickly take measures, because the house is collapsing." All of them — from Gorbachev to the weaver. Like shamans, lurching with their drums around a fire. *'Oof, oof, we will hunt the bear, oof oof, let it be a clear day.'* Not one of them dared to see the simple truth: the foundation is rotten, everything has to be built anew, and the building cannot be of a hundred stories. Solzhenitsyn is able to see this from the far reaches of Vermont, but these people are drawing their hats down over their eyes. They do not see not because they are stupid, but because they do not dare to take a look. They would then have to admit they are unnecessary.

The president of the Soviet Union then completely blew it in his speech. He expressed doubt regarding the results of the elections in the Ukraine, the desire of the Georgians, and, of course, of the Baltics. "We have to take another look at how the voting there went, and what the voting was for." Does this need comment? But why should we hold back from commenting from modesty? We know how we voted and for what. And, by the way, who voted for Gorbachev? He even became a deputy by simply appointing himself as one. And he became president by the votes of those similarly appointed and "elected" in Tmutarakan. If he were to offer himself today as a candidate to the people of Russia, like Yelcin is planning to offer himself, I wonder if he would get even fifteen percent of the vote.

Even under these conditions, the president is taking all power unto himself. Which means, of course, he is also assuming all of the responsibility. Germany will send butter and canned food which was lying in storage waiting for a blockade of Berlin, and Italy will send macaroni. Another wooden two by four to prop up the hundred story structure.

The Soviet Union, rich in everything that God can give, especially in people longing to live like people, had its chance in this giant railroad station named History.

The Hungarian train waited a long time in that station. The Soviet Union came too late and missed it.

The train "Poland" rumbled merrily like a Cossack into the train yard. The Soviet Union looked the other way and then it was too late.

21

Breaking across walls, in sped the train "East Germany." "Ah, what do you Germans know?" It rolled down the line, on the way picking up kalashinkovs and deserters. In three years it will demonstrate an economic miracle.

Into the railroad station drew the chariot "Czechoslovakia": elegant, with velvet lining. It was ignored.

Now the platform is quiet and empty. Neither sausages, nor beer. And it waxes ever colder.

From the depo in the distance still can be seen the steam from yet one last train. Its boiler hisses as the vapors heat. It is the last and final train. And upon it in large letters is written the word: "Ceaucescu."

* * *

Algimantas Čekuolis, born 1931 in Lithuania, was the editor in 1990 of the then most popular and respected weekly newspaper in Lithuania, *Gimtasis kraštas*. He at the time was also a deputy to the Supreme Soviet of the Soviet Union. Čekuolis appeared on many Western television news programs as an unofficial commentator on events in Lithuania. The original article appeared in *Gimtasis kraštas* #47 (1236). Vilnius, November 22-28, 1990. This translation was published in *Lituanus*, the Lithuanian Quarterly Journal of Arts and Sciences, Vol. 37, No.1 (Spring 1991).

ROMANCE ON A BUS

Pulgis Andriušis

Translated by Tadas Klimas

One can catch the flavor of those by-gone, pre-World War II summer days in Lithuania. The story ends with an unusual twist on the theme of boy-meets-girl. Or rather, schmuck-meets-girl.

Today the Birštonas-Kaunas bus was carrying a sleepy and nearly full load of passengers. The bus driver had apparently had a few drinks at the bus station to ensure a lucky trip. Driving though the forests, he had tried to exchange a few jokes with his passengers, but not having received any encouragement, he had now given himself over completely to that epidemic of sadness which was devastating those inhabitants of Kaunas, the temporary capital, who had had to interrupt their lazy summer days in the resort town of Birštonas to return for a time to the grey mundaneity of everyday life.

Bringing to mind the recuperating nature of Birštonas, it wasn't surprising that the majority of passengers were of a somewhat advanced, solid, age: a trio of officers who had undone their stiff collars, a podgy priest completely engrossed in a holy book, a couple of businessmen in their black cylindrical hats, a few women in black dresses, one of whom sported a no longer stylish crocheted shawl — all of them together solid citizenry of the temporary capital, bureaucrats, contractors, landlords, for whom it was just the time, to seriously concern themselves with that old rheumatism, arthritis, or other statements of account presented to those of advanced years. And so all the hooks and mesh shelving of the bus were filled with indescribable, to a healthy person bewildering, orthopedic appliances.

A young blonde girl was sitting by herself next to a window, wearing a handsomely knitted blue dress. She was reading a French novel, and from time to time lifted her head to gaze at the end-of-summer birches and fields. The late season sun, twisting through the glades, gaily played on the girl's light tresses, bringing out the summer's tanned oval of her face in all its beauty. On the corner hook there hung all folded out a jacket of foreign manufacture; apparently under its jutting angles were deposited all necessaries for the road. In the netting above contentedly reposed this beautiful girl's smartly beribboned suitcase and she had covered her knees with a travel blanket of unfamiliar pattern. The blonde was truly the pride of the bus, the only flower amongst dried-out brushwood.

The bus stopped for a short time in Prienai, just long enough for the nimble bus driver to drink down while standing a couple of mugs of the renowned local beer and to board a few new passengers. Just before the bus took off, a not very tall student jumped in, bedecked in the full panoply of fraternal ornaments and ribbons, all ready to celebrate *initium semestri* or other inanities. The setting sun flashed against the gold and silver in his cap, the woven ribbon across his chest, the freshly pressed vest, the healthy milk and blood of his face. Prienai setting out to conquer Kaunas!

The bus driver rejoiced in having found such an agile person to converse with and showed the collegiate an empty seat near him. But the beer-town academic, before sitting down, gazed like a conqueror over the entourage. When, however, his vision took in the blonde it stumbled and he suddenly lost all his cock-of-the-walk boldness. Waving the bus driver into silence, with the back of his hand, he meekly approached the girl and asked if he could sit by her. She, breaking off from her book, almost imperceptibly inclined her head, remarking,

"It's an unnecessary question. The seat belongs to anyone who has a ticket."

The student's face, having just been milk and blood, now betrayed no trace of milk but was red all the way up to the ears. He barely managed to stammer out,

"Well, anyway, I thought it couldn't hurt to ask . . ."

"I appreciate politeness, even when unnecessary," replied the lovely passenger, "It's only forced courtesy I dislike. Well, where are you travelling to?"

She spoke those last words in so friendly and open a manner that the Prienai dandy felt at once that his conqueror's weapons were unneeded here, conforming his earlier impression formed after a quick glance at the French novel in her lap, her exotic baggage and her tasteful clothing. The collegiate, having recovered his color, now spoke with her as if she were an old friend. Following his Dzukian predilection he told her all about the ball his fraternity was hosting that night. The student had fallen in love with this rare beauty at first sight, and now showered her with questions, burning with curiosity to discover as much as possible about her. He was prepared to slow down or even to stop the bus, which hurried on by the bored driver, inescapedly sped towards journey's end.

"Are you a student, Miss?" he asked, looking at her French book.

"Yes. I study people, life . . ." she answered with a sad smile, brushing back a golden tress that had fallen across the bronze oval of her face.

Noticing how intently the student's eyes were studying her suitcase, covered as it were with colorful stickers of foreign hotels, the blonde began to tell of her travels throughout Europe. The ears of the lad from a Dzukian one-horse town rang with Romantic names of Mediterranean cities, of the Alps, of the Black Forest.

Our frat-man, not having been farther than Karaliaučiai and Riga, bewitched by those names of far places, slumped in his seat, realizing that his wings were too short for such flights, inasmuch as the resources of his father, a Prienai shopkeeper, only just permitted him to continue his studies in Kaunas.

The bus flew past Garliava, annoying the local ducks, and then slowed up at the large hill of Aleksotas. The student realized the situation demanded fast and determined action if this interesting acquaintanceship were not to remain only an autumn journey's pleasant memory.

"A first meeting is perhaps not a sufficient cause," he began, wanting to invite her to that evening's college-style ball, but the girl did not let him finish his sentence. She just smiled even more touchingly and softly remarked,

"A first meeting is sometimes also the last . . ."

The youth jumped to his feet to protest passionately. But the bus was already turning into the final stop in the old town, and the passengers were jostling one another, getting their baggage, putting on their coats. Now was the time for lightning actions, not for words. Charge! The collegiate politely offered and was grabbing the girl's things, saying he'd hire a taxi for her in the station yard. But the girl, without making a move from her seat into the confusion, unexpectedly and strongly objected,

"No, no, you get off first and perhaps give me a hand outside, but right now the driver will take care of me — we've already agreed!"

Into her smile now stole perhaps even a hint of mockery, which the student lacked the time to notice.

Burning with envy of the bus driver, the student waited impatiently in the station yard until the last person got off the bus. He was about to jump back in when on the bus steps appeared she of his dreams, assigned him by fate . . . leaning on two crutches.

The college-boy disappeared into the crowd.

* * *

Pulgis Andriušis (born 1907 in Lithuania; died 1970 in Australia) was a journalist, translator, and editor. He was active in the Esperanto movement and was widely traveled. He translated Cervantes' *Don Quixote* into Lithuanian. Pulgis Andriušis' works were collected and published in at least two collections by clubs in the United States, and recently at least one collection has been printed in Lithuania. This translation was published in *Lituanus*, the Lithuanian Quarterly Journal of Arts and Sciences, Vol. 31, No. 1 (Spring 1985).

DRIVEN OUT

Jurgis Jankus

Translated by Tadas Klimas

I used to be able to tell the time, to the minute, by looking up at the sky. I had developed the ability during several summers of working out of doors.

What if you had spent your life working a farm, amongst neighbors doing the same? Would you not have grown into your land, your home? And then what would happen if foreign armies were to invade, bent upon expanding cruel and inhuman regimes? Would you not consider fleeing? Could you stay? Or would you have been driven out, from home?

Light rain was falling like a fine mist. Clouds descended to the tops of the pines, and the smell of dampness covered branches of trees, roofs of houses, and the well-worked fields of Kalnėnai. Everywhere in the air, in every little branch of pine, even in the gray drops hanging on the needles of the pines, everything was full of silence. Nothing disturbed it. Neither a bird nor an animal was heard, not even the baying of a dog. Along the fringes of the forest, along the sandy road, with their wagons filled to overflowing, moved the ones who were running away. But even their going did not disturb the quiet, which had covered as if with silver veil that whole peaceful little corner nestled among the pines. The runaways not only did not speak among themselves but also did not urge the horses on out loud, as if afraid someone might hear and stop them.

Andrius Blažys leaned on the picket fence and looked toward the edge of the forest. He hadn't closed his eyes all night. The last three months everything had quieted down so much, it seemed it might just go on this way until the Germans would bring together more forces to bear down upon the Russians and would push them back. Still, there had been nothing to indicate they were indeed getting ready to do something.

Until yesterday afternoon. Explosions, such as he had never heard before in his life. Not even in the First World War, not even a couple years ago, when at the break of dawn the iron might of the Germans had rolled like a dreadnought toward the East. Then there had been shooting, a tremendous amount of shooting, but yesterday they had roared like a cloud of ice. All of a sudden they had roared and roared — and then had died away. Everything had become quiet and had stayed that way. The idea had come to mind this storm had not come from the side of the Bolsheviks but that it was the Germans who had halted the movement of the other side. Although his son says it was the others who had crushed the German front, what does he know. If it had been crushed they would have been here long ago. They are not so stupid to wait until the Germans recover. So it was probably they themselves who had gotten hit.

Wrestling with such thoughts, he had tossed about on his bed until midnight, when he had risen to take a look around and had been astonished to discover that the entire patch of sky between his stand of pines and the state forest far off to the left was lit and gleaming with separate fires. He had counted fifteen and then, having walked around his stand of pines, he had counted twenty-three more. And there was no sound to be heard other than that of the flames racing heavenward. "That's what happens to people's toil and sweat," he said out loud to himself in the silence of the night. "Well, if you really want to fight, then fight, go crazy, beat each other to death, but why do you torture people? Don't you know there are more than just

Germans and Russians living in this world?[1] There are also people. How have they sinned against anyone?"

With these words he left the corner of the pines and returned to lean upon his fence. He stood there, leaning and chasing one thought after another — but also from time to time without thought, simply holding on, alone with his. unease.

As the gray of dawn became lighter, he felt his wife come out of their cottage and again he spoke out loud:

"So what do they have to go for? Flocking as if to the festival of St. Rokas. It's so peaceful ... If the others had broken through, they would have been here long ago. They're probably running again. You can't see the smoke through the fog, but last night all the houses over there were burning. And look how they're forcing the animals across the sandy lands! They could wait right here until it was time to go back. But even then. And where do they think they're going? What do they think they'll find, when Satan has already laid everything to waste over there. People will have to live on bare fields."

He talked, but he himself could not really say to whom he was saying these words, because saying them he did not even look toward his wife.

"We know why they are going," she answered. Looking too at the forest edge. "If he said that the German front has been crushed, then that's the way it is. The Germans themselves told him that. Maybe they're sneaking out through the forests quietly, so that fewer people would run. Why they're running we all know, but what they'll find only God himself knows.

---

[1] Trans. note: Lithuania was invaded and occupied by the Soviet Union, then Nazi Germany's ally, at the start of WWII. Subsequently, Germany invaded Lithuania (and swept away a government which the Lithuanians had re-created as the Soviets had fled or been repulsed). Eventually the Soviet Union re-invaded Lithuania and held it until the re-establishment (again) of independence in 1990, recognized by Western democracies in 1991.

Obviously, there's no one waiting to welcome anyone there. Who doesn't know that it isn't good to leave one's home, to leave everything, but the heart does not decide that. Even if you stay, what's to be done, when your house is no longer yours, your work is no longer yours. Even if they don't turn it to ashes, they'll put someone else here in our place, and then they'll just load us up and ship us off. Like the last time. As if we've forgotten . . . Us, we're just us. Even if they take us away, our days are numbered anyway, but the children. Surely among people we wouldn't perish."

From afar the woman tried gingerly to turn the talk in her direction, but a sudden anger seized the old man. He turned away from the fence and stared at her with his gray, time-bleached, eyes.

"Don't talk to me about your 'people!' As if anyone is waiting to welcome you there with cakes. Run! Bolt! Go like crazy! Grab up your skirts and run! Like the freaky winds. You're all the same. Just run, just scatter everything along the sides. Everything! To the last crumb!"

He wasn't talking anymore but was shouting so loud even the dew soaked pine forest echoed. And he wasn't shouting any longer at his wife, for in the middle of his words he had turned again to the fence. He didn't lean on it; instead he grasped the posts with both hands, so hard that his knuckles were white, and he shouted to the fields and forests, so loudly that probably even those who were still moving along the edge of the forest heard. So that all those might hear who of their own will would leave their homes to go out and scatter everything away.

To leave. To emptiness. To nothingness. From here, where for sixty years he had broken apart every larger clod of dirt, where he had turned this sandy pine-producing sand-soil into fertile earth. Oh that one should . . . that you should . . .

The wife quietly stepped away inside; so quietly, even the door made no sound. She put her arms around her daughter and both of them looked through the fogged up window to the East, from whence came destruction. Unstoppable, implacable, like death itself. Through that same window she herself had seen the fires in the night. When one had started to die out, soon another had lifted its flames to the sky, as if the world itself had caught afire.

"If someone would come and tell us how it would really be, then we'd know if we should leave everything and go, or if we should fold our hands and wait until everything stops roaring," she said, and not to her daughter, but straight to the pane of glass.

She looked at the bent back of her husband, who was still standing by the fence. Pain tore at her heart. Her life had seen it torn more than once. When her daughter had died, when the Russians had deported her son. It had torn even more deeply when the Germans had found the mutilated body of her son in the NKVD garage.[2] It had torn deeply then, but in a different way. Then it had torn from loss, but now it was tearing because man is so paltry a thing, so powerless, and against what? Against that self-same man. Without moving her lips she whispered, "Dear Lord, if this hour I did not have these living ones I would have no worry, my heart would not even ache. I would give myself up to your will and would just sit here. Let be what must be. But, why, You Yourself have placed them all in my weak hands? The children and my husband, who also has a heart, but who just doesn't want to open it. Oh God, oh God!" she quietly lamented, so softly even her daughter could barely hear.

"It's as quiet as a Sunday morning," Kęstutis, the last living son of the Blažys family, interrupted his mother's thoughts as he

---

[2] Transl. note: The NKVD was the predecessor of the later Soviet-era KGB, the Soviet secret police.

came in through the door. "The birds are all gone, the shepherds are sleeping, and what the Germans and the Russians are doing only they know."

He had been like this from early youth. Whatever subject he would touch he would turn it on its side, would make a joke, would even turn his own pain into laughter. These words of his rendered his mother and sister even more sorrow-stricken, and they could not find words with which to answer him. The house grew even more silent than the outdoors; only the pendulum of the old wall clock continued to tick rhythmically and mundanely, but this ticking just served to accentuate the silence.

The son stood a while. He touched a colorful rug that had been placed on a bench, and then said,

"The weather is warm, the mist is heavy, the fog drizzles along the ground — there will be plenty of mushrooms. Even tomorrow we'll be able to gather baskets full of them."

He spoke unconcernedly and even with a slight smile on his lips. But he realized at once how out of place this was and his voice trembled anxiously of itself.

"Have you finished harnessing the horses?" his sister asked. Her voice was also soft: burdened, like a sigh, as if she were afraid someone might hear.

"I harnessed a team. We'll be able to start out and speed right along to the church festival. St. Simon-Jude's. Did you see that the sacristan has been burning candles from midnight already? Hope we make it on time for High Mass. I don't want to get there only to put out the candles."

The mother suddenly turned from the window and looked at her son. It had struck her that a healthy person does not talk like this. Could the child be getting confused? But Kęstutis was looking very calmly through another window, not at all like a madman would. Except that his face was pale, and his lips were trembling, as if he were striving with all his might to hold back the tears. And perhaps words as well. Not such as he had spoken but totally different. The kind he usually kept to himself.

Then she turned, came up close to him, and put her hand on her child's shoulder. Not the whole hand, but just the tips of her work thickened fingers. She wanted to tell him to go to his father and talk to him man to man. If everyone is going, and if the Germans had placed cannon at the edge of the pine forest, no good is to come anyway. She was still searching for words when her son began to speak just as if he were still talking about gathering mushrooms.

"Look at father. He's dug a hole all by himself, and now he wants to put a roof over it to keep the rain off."

"Kęstutis, dear son, how can you talk like that at a time like this ..."

Kęstutis grasped his mother's fingers with a firm grip and said, "I'm sorry, Mama, I didn't mean it angrily, but when — "

His voice broke off, his face trembled, his mouth twisted convulsively. Now. they stood, holding each other. It was completely light outside and they could clearly see the wagons working their way along the edge of the forest. It was even possible now to recognize who it was that was going. A group of German soldiers trudged through the fringe of the pine forest. Not like people but like colored shadows. One of them stepped to the side and came up to the people in the wagons: he said something and hurried back to the other soldiers. He had probably ordered the people in the wagons to move faster, because one of the men the soldier had spoken to immediately pulled on the reins and the horses jumped into a trot. In that same moment the father turned from the fence and inspected the ditch. He shoveled the dirt in several places where it had been dug up out of the ditch and tossed it further away. He

35

looked about as if wanting to be sure no one was coming to help him, then he pushed his hat back and turned toward the barn, where piles of wood were stacked in a shed.

The ditch he had begun to dig a long time ago, as soon as he had heard that the Russians had reached Kaunas.

"What for?" Kęstutis had joked. "Do you think they will come here to fight? One morning you'll just wake up and there'll be a chekist behind the door. "Hey, tovarisch! Get dressed," he'll say, "and *paidiom* to Siberia." But his father had told Kęstutis first to wipe the mother's milk from his lips and only then to teach his father.

"Do you think the Germans will let them come into their country so easily? You'll see what happens when they come this far. I know what happened during the first one. Not only did people crawl into holes themselves, but they dug them for their animals as well. Otherwise many of them would have wound up dead. When I get dug in, into this earth, let them fight for weeks. Let them fight as much as they want. Now, none of you want to lift a finger to help me, but when things get rough, you'll come. And how you'll come. Crawling for your lives." That was what he had said then: now he pulled beams out from under the roof. Thick ones, planed on two sides. The same ones he had been planning, just before the Russians had come, to use in building a special small kitchen at the end of the stables, so they wouldn't have to prepare fodder for the animals in the dwelling house. But when they had come, when suddenly everything had become no longer one's own, he had left the beams for a better time. Now he gathered them to cover his hole.

Kęstutis turned from the window.

"Father dug himself a hole right here, but where have we?" he began. "Maybe it will be like he said: we'll all fit there until the NKVD types arrive and pull us out, one by one."

36

His voice was now dark, heavy, and cold as ice. So cold, if you pierced your heart itself with his frost, you would feel no pain. It would freeze even the pain.

"What's the matter with you today? Enough, Kęstutis! Be a human. Go, talk to him. He doesn't listen to us, but he'll surely listen to you. He can't want what happened to Vytukas to happen to you," again his mother urged him.

"He won't listen, Mama. I talked to him; last night I talked to him. He ordered me to stay, too. He said, the Russians will have learned and will return different from the way they were. He won't listen. Do you think it was easy for me to watch him drag those beams all by himself? If he would listen, I'd help him, but he won't listen anymore. It seems the time has arrived when we each listen to ourselves. Do you think it's easy for me to be leaving here? Don't imagine that when they get here they will quickly leave. This time hiding in the forest won't work for me. Then again, perhaps. Perhaps father is right, but something keeps telling me that a dog once stepped upon is more apt to bite. And when those return they'll bite. They'll tear & rend like mad, but will father understand that? You know, Mama, it's not easy for me to leave here, but he, through his entire life, has merged from head to toe with this sandy land. Where can I find such a word that he would heed? He simply is unable to throw everything aside and leave. But everything is packed. We could have easily driven away last night already; the border, they say, is open, but how can we leave him alone? How? Mama, how can we leave father here all alone?"

He fell silent. The mother did not speak. Neither did the two sisters. All of them watched as the father took a beam, heaved it over his shoulder, and, as if bent under a heavy cross, walked through the yard.

"You get ready," Kęstutis suddenly decided. "I'll help carry the wood; we'll cover the top of the hole. At least I'll help that much, and then we leave. No one can say how much time there is left. Father is immovable, but I won't leave any of you."

He stepped toward the door, but the mother caught his hand.

"Then I'll stay here, too," she stated. "How can we leave him here all alone, like something I don't know what. You young people, who would ..."

From the eastern side a machine gun sounded, very close by, as if someone had strewn steel peas on a tin roof. The morning's quiet was suddenly torn apart, and all of them started so violently that the mother's last word broke off in her throat. The father stopped for a moment and turned his head towards the side of the shooting. Soon after the first, a second and the third volley burst out, as if answering each other. The father then quickened his pace and almost in a run approached the gate, where the end of the beam became caught in the branches of the cherry tree. Tearing his way through he loudly cursed that everywhere he has to do everything by himself, that if it weren't for his bloody sweat, they all would have seen an end long ago.

Having come up to the hole, he put the beam down and wiped his sweat. The shooting died down. It broke off just as suddenly as it had started. Even from far off the father's face showed concern, whether he will have time, all by himself, to carry enough beams to cover the hole. And he had thought to cover it with a double layer. First width-wise, and then length-wise, so as to withstand even a direct hit.

"I'm going," said Kęstutis, letting go of his mother's hand.

Perhaps he wanted to say something more, perhaps he wanted to say he would not leave her for anything, but he was cut off by a piercing sound, like a violent sneeze. A sound to make one's insides shake.

"Oh Jesus!" screamed the mother, crouching down near her son's feet. Petrutė jumped from the window and grabbed the patterned rug from the bench, as if she could shield herself with it.

"It's only the German cannon, nothing to be scared about," Kęstutis calmed them. "It's only the start. They, it seems, are trying to slow the Russians. Mama, get up. It's time. Now no home will keep us safe. Not even father's ditch. Let's go. I'll take him in my arms and carry him like a baby. Otherwise I'll never get him out of here."

He helped his mother get up, but suddenly there was a flash of light and a blast that shattered the window, its pieces landing on the floor and on the bench. Through the window he saw the falling beam his father had placed upright at the side of the hole. It seemed to him his father had purposely pushed the beam forward and had himself toppled over backwards. With one leap Kęstutis was through the door, but his father no longer needed help. He lay on the freshly shoveled sand with his head thrown back in an uncomfortable position, as if he wanted to see what was back of his head. But he had nothing left to see with. In place of his eyes and his furrowed brow there was only a formless, splattered mass, from which only now did blood begin to seep.

The son knelt down upon one knee, took one of his father's lifeless hands and looked for a time at his face, of which was left only the narrow, taut lips and several days' growth of stubble on his chin.

Russian cannon thundered from the other side of the forest, missiles flew overhead, some exploding further off in the pines, others right by the houses; the Sunday quiet was completely torn apart. But Kęstutis did not really hear all that. He, with both hands, placed his father's head in a more normal position. He then stood up and looked about, as if unable to think of what more he should do. His mother and sisters were already

39

standing next to him, speechless. He hadn't felt their arrival. Petrutė still held the rug clutched in her embrace, pressing it with both hands to her chest. She was the first to speak.

"Do you need some help?"

Her words woke Kęstutis up as if from sleep. He lifted up his head and took a quick look around.

"Okay, help. Bring a saw and an axe."

When his sister was near the door, he turned to the youngest.

"And you, Stepute, run to the storehouse. Under the window in a box there are some nails. Bring two of the biggest. No, take three," he corrected himself.

As the girl ran off, he spread on the ground Petrutė's colorful rug that she had dropped there, picked up his father, and placed him upon it. He wrapped him up in it, then picked him up and climbed down into the ditch. He laid him down on the floor that had been carefully evened and covered with boards.

The mother, kneeling at the edge of the ditch, began to pray. Kęstutis and Petrutė sawed off a length of beam and then sawed crosswise upon it: with several blows of the axe, Kęstutis split the shards away and made a nest, then pressed the beams together and hammered three large nails into them, so that they would really hold. He took up the whole heavy cross and set it in the hole past his father's head. He told Stepute to hold it, and he and Petrutė began to shovel earth back into the hole until in its place was a mound of sand. There were no thoughts in his mind, but all of him felt as if someone had nailed his feet to the spot. When he lifted his head again, everything was quiet again. No missiles whistled, no bombs burst. And the German cannon that had been at the edge of the forest were no longer to be seen. While they were working at their father's grave, the cannon had disappeared somewhere.

"Let's go!" he said glancing once more across the fields.

He took his mother by the hand. She almost stumbled. Petrutė jumped to her other side. Steputė ran ahead towards the barn, where the horses had been standing harnessed since dawn. Kęstutis seated the women and jumped up himself. He pulled on the reins and they were off. They didn't even turn back to close the barn doors. In any case, soon others would be opening and closing them. Or perhaps not — just beyond the stand of pines the buildings of the Stirna family were already afire, sending smoke and flame up to the clouds that still hung just above the rooftops.

With her right hand, the mother made the sign of the cross over the farmstead and her sweat soaked fields. Kęstutis kept urging the horses to a brisk trot. They were completely alone; no one was to be seen either before or behind them, as if they were in the middle of a big emptiness. Only after a few kilometers, when they drove out of the forest, did they see the highway to the right. German army vehicles still crowded the highway, and not all of them were heading west. From time to time one or two were seen speeding towards the east.

They could hear cannon fire start up again behind them, but no missiles flew overhead. Kęstutis slowed the horses, which had begun to overheat, to a walk. At the Šerksna stream he halted them completely.

"What happened?" asked Petrutė, who was sitting next to him.

Kęstutis lifted up his hands. They were bloody with the blood of his father.

"When I wanted to straighten his head —" he said, then got down from the wagon and washed off the last part of his father in the stream. When he had begun to drive again, he said,

"He used to say there are more than just Nazis and Bolsheviks in the world, people, without whom the world would not be the world. People who plant, who grow things, who don't destroy anything, who work so not only today but tomorrow would be better. And there, there was a person, but they came from somewhere and crushed him like a flea. They don't even know they crushed him. Like nothing, like he had never existed."

The women remained silent. They just stood there and from time to time wiped away their tears. Kęstutis fell silent, too. He had no idea whether he had succeeded in putting into words that of which not only he but the entire world seemed full to bursting. At least it seemed to him that it was full.

* * *

Jurgis Jankus was born in Lithuania in 1906. He already enjoyed an excellent reputation as a novelist in pre-war Lithuania when he had to flee his homeland to escape the Soviet occupation. Settling in Rochester, New York, he worked in factories and raised four boys with his wife, Kotryna. He wrote at night and on the weekends, and published a number of collections of short stories and two plays. In 1991 he traveled to Lithuania, which had newly re-established its independence, for the first time since WWII. There he greatly enjoyed the many literary events which were organized in his honor. Jurgis Jankus died in 2002 and is buried in Rochester, New York.

This story's original title in Lithuanian is *Iš Namų*. It was originally published in a collection of short stories by Jurgis Jankus, *Paparčio žiedas* (Lietuviškos knygos klubas 1982 [393 pages]), which won the 1981 Lithuanian American Community, Inc., prize for literature. This translation, under the title *From Home*, was published in *Lituanus*, the Lithuanian Quarterly Journal of Arts and Sciences, Vol. 33, No. 2 (Summer 1987).

An excerpt from a contemporary review of the original Lithuanian-language version:

The collection starts with the story, 'Iš Namų,' which is not burdened by any unwarranted additions. For here the author speaks sparingly, and this reserve wins one over. We understand the characters as we would ourselves. We don't have to know Blažys' past, nor about his relatives, nor of any hijinks he may have gotten into back when. It is enough to learn about the situation, and the reader sympathizes with the old man's decision, which is expressed in just a couple short dialogues. His decision describes him in full, a farmer who cannot be parted from his land "... over the course of his life he had entirely, from head to toe, grown into those sandy fields." ... One doesn't have to read many pages to weigh the pain of Blažys' wife, torn between him and his son. And it is similarly irrelevant whether their son, Kęstutis, kas already graduated college, or whether he is a student, or just a grown-up young farmer. Having already been hiding in the woods from the bolsheviks, he is a clear candidate for deportation to Siberia or the the next world without us having to know more details about him. The hellish environment is also brought forth without long descriptions: the roads are filled with refugees, fleeing their homes; the death of Blažys and his horrific burial. ... 'Iš Namų' [Driven Out] is the best story in the collection.[3]

---

[3] Vytautas Dyvas (pseudonym of Vytautas Volertas], *Ilga Pasaka Trumpa Tiesą* (*Aidai*, 1983/4 liepa-rugpjūtis) (available at http://aidai.us/index.php?option=com_content&task=view&id=7301&Itemid=478). Quoted material translated by Tadas Klimas.

SIGITAS GEDA'S ADDRESS TO LITHUANIA

GIVEN JULY 9, 1988 IN VINGIS PARK, VILNIUS, LITHUANIA

Sigitas Geda

Translated by Tadas Klimas

The Address was delivered before a crowd of 700,000 by perhaps Lithuania's greatest poet, Sigitas Geda. It was given on the occasion of a mass public reception of the Lithuanian delegates to the 19th Congress of the Soviet Union's Communist Party. Many of the people in the crowd were carrying the tricolor flag of independent Lithuania which was as yet illegal, although it was also the flag of the Lithuanian Restructuring Movement, the organizer of the event. The Lithuanian Restructuring Movement has as its goal a national renewal for Lithuania, including autonomy from Moscow in economics and culture. The July 9, 1988 demonstration was a signal event, incontrovertibly proving the strength of the Lithuanian identity and consciousness in the face of decades of Russification and oppression.

Dear Lithuanians and all whom the earth of Lithuania upholds with welcome! We need mighty manifestations with which to shake Lithuania's bureaucracy with every step. Perhaps it will, when it starts to think of other things, return to its senses. Then things will be different. But now let us start from this, that each of us has or has not a larger or smaller apartment, a house, a roof above our heads, a corner or a yard, to which we will have to return this evening or tomorrow, to our parents, brother's, and sisters, children, and to others whom we hold dear. What will we say to them, what will we say even to ourselves, when we are alone with ourselves; what will we say to those, who have returned to eternal peace today, yesterday or the day before, who lie in the holy earth of Lithuania and even further — in all the places of the earth: In Yakutsk and Udmurdia, not far from the Arctic Circle, and right here unjustly shot to death in the dark and dreadful courtyards of Vilnius or its half-cellars.[1] We will say to them we are one of the oldest nations, that we had a giant country and did not have the strength to preserve it, that we survived an endless number of national desecrations, occupations, revolts, exiles, and reawakenings.

Yet is this the way to speak with the living and the dead?

All of this would be but beautiful and sad poetry. But it is more important now to say to them that even this final patch of ground does not lie secure beneath our feet, but we will strive to brace ourselves more firmly upon it, so we could, honestly and nobly and simply, live — and die, should it come to that, in the same way as would the whole world and as every nation, an honorable nation among honorable nations, as the last swimmers from a sinking Noah's ark who do not give way to panic.

We have many opportunities to swim our way out. We only have to gather that which belonged to our fathers and grandfathers: our things and our toys, our flags, our books, our churches and all of our reliquaries. And let no one interfere. Because in the final analysis we are all equally miserable wretches. But it is most important for all of us to remember we have each a singular, immortal and unique soul. I am not saying that each of us, brought up as atheists or agnostics, cynics, pragmatics, or nihilists, from tomorrow onward should begin to believe in God; however, one of the paramount reasons why today Lithuanians are so timid, skeptical, lost and apathetic is because we have all grown up under the shadow of Satan. Only through a higher — let us not be afraid to say it — a cosmic purpose for man have the wide world's cultures, nations, and civilizations been able to bear any fruit. Immortal works of art have been created, churches erected, homes, manors, and the

---

[1] Refers to the deportation to Siberia of 250,000 Lithuanians in an effort to subdue resistance to Soviet rule. Also refers to a similar number executed by Soviet security forces in Lithuania itself.

cottages of our fathers have been built, all in this belief: that man has a higher, spiritual nature. In this belief, men have not feared to die in the name of their country. To make offerings and sacrifices.

We must descry a higher and purer origin for the life around us in order to be able to defend it. Is this foreign to modern civilization, to twentieth century technocracy, and to the forthcoming future of computers and superconductors? Absolutely not. Our misfortune is that which has been and which is being created in Lithuania is a tasteless and unclean monstrosity. Our glorified cosmopolitan architecture is a monstrosity; our much-lauded collective farms are monstrosities; monstrosities, too, are our acclaimed factories and power plants; monstrosities as well are our own clanking, constantly under repair and irreparable, automobiles. A grotesque conglomeration of the relics of socialism and capitalism threatens us, as it does many wrongly oriented central and eastern European countries.

In each step, in each of our words and deeds, we must seek that our activity and function would turn to plastic, and plastic to the spiritual — a unit of beauty and goodness. Such a perspective civilization I saw in Japan, which in its deep coordination of the ancient, middle, and modern ages reminded me of Lithuania. Something similar could have developed in Lithuania's neighbor, Finland, if its fathers' legacy, traditions, characters, and predilections would not have been made foul by a tasteless Americanism.

Much that is foreign and dangerous to Lithuania could be repeated here from defiled socialist Poland. Greatly esteeming that country, with which we are connected not only by many injuries, but also with many fine perceptions, I cannot quietly witness her drama, her convulsive bewilderment in the present.

We must search for our own road, remaining faithful to our customs and traditions, our cultural legacy. We must return once again to the strongest of strong castles and citadels — to Lithuanian minds, that we would not survive as a third-rate nation, but as a unique nation among nations, a sovereign nation among sovereign nations.

Often I have spoken and written that I do not like the status of an aborigine, that I do not want to live in Lithuania like in some kind of Zulu reservation.

Let us be wary of those who always stress we are a nation of tillers of the soil, of those who wish to remind us we have no need of a high human identity, nor of our own political and military public figures, our own industrial, academic, and union leaders, our own pilots and helmsmen, our own nuclear energy specialists and our own astronauts. Hundreds of years before Ciolkovski, Lithuanians had Simanavičius, and in 1933 — Darius and Girėnas, who proved we are capable not only of accepting from the world, but also of bestowing upon it, examples of intelligence, nobility, strength, and honor.[2]

Drive forth from the vocabularies of our serious and frivolous, learned and unschooled men and women the deluded reassurance: "We are a small nation." (The crowd chants *Lie-tu-va!* — the Lithuanian name for Lithuania.)

Even before the war, Balys Sruoga said, if a nation is large, then it has within it many fools.[3] But if a nation is small . . . what if it is that way, regardless? In this aspect of the world, it would be gainful to remember an Indian tale about a mouse and an elephant — this is not mine, but the wisdom of one of my friends, living and dead: "The mouse will never conquer the elephant, but at the fateful moment it can run up inside the

[2] Kazimieras Simanovičius (?1600-?1660) wrote a book on rockets & artillery, long considered the principal work on the subject. Lithuanian-Americans Darius & Girėnas daringly flew a single engine plane across the Atlantic in 1933.
[3] Balys Sruoga (1896-1947), Lithuanian poet, dramatist and scholar.

elephant's trunk and tickle it, so that this terribly swelled up gerbil will begin to sneeze like crazy." Or a Japanese insight: "Can a skinny fellow, let us say Lithuania, overwhelm a giant?" Yes, absolutely yes. One just has to seize the moment when the giant is balanced upon the toe.

And also in Lithuania, even before the war, one of our most eminent historians, Ignas Jonynas, deduced the reason why Lithuania needs Vilnius.[4] Is it only that "We will never quit without Vilnius!" No, with Vilnius we inherit the cultural tradition of the ancient Lithuania state, but with only Kaunas we would be reduced to such a status as Estonia and Latvia. This is why Vilnius, in the words of Oscar Milosz,[5] is the Athens of the North; why our friend and contemporary the Hungarian A. Boitaras can quietly sigh, "Only through the history of Lithuania is it possible to fully discover and explain much of the history of Central and Eastern Europe, because it is the fullest and most independent historical model." Vilnius to Lithuania is necessary with each of its churches and monasteries, orthodox churches & madrasahs.[6] And certainly with its synagogue or synagogues, because Vilnius is a holy city for that other nation floundering in a diaspora, the Jews. Vilnius is of European cities, one of the six most beautiful, before and after Amsterdam. Vilnius is for us and for the world. And all of this Geda heaps upon our poor socialist shoulders? All of these Utopias in our run down, silicon, collective-farmed Lithuania, where there is so much fear, so much darkness, so many unsettled accounts. Where an atheist can have no dialogue with a believer, a Communist with a non-party person, a Lithuanian with a Russian, a Russian with a Pole and a Tatar? Yes, here, because here is the only place we have to live and die, to

---

[4] Vilnius, although undeniably part of Lithuania and indeed its ancient capital city, was treacherously invaded by Poland in 1919. Vilnius remained occupied by Poland until World War Two.

[5] Oscar Milosz (1877-1939), Lithuanian poet and diplomat who wrote in French.

[6] A madrasah is an institution of higher learning attached to a mosque.

redeem real and non-existant transgressions, to rot with bones irradiated by Chernobyl and Ignalina.[7]

But before that we need new learned men and women, new diplomats, new jurists and economists. We need doors open to the whole world — to the universities of Cracow, Berlin, Munich, Freiburg and Friburg, Grenoble, Rome and Paris. Russians, Latvians, and Ukrainians need these, too. This is a matter which the great nation must attend to at once.

We need a new type of priest in the line of Vaižgantas and Putinas[8], who would replace their fellows who have become merely compromised psychiatrists. We need a belief in truth, heart, and love — but paramountly a new, deep, and fundamental belief in the higher calling of man on earth.

In this light I would like to see those, who stand here young and beautiful, who will live on after us, and we will be able to withdraw with peaceful hearts.

As my last word, I have the honor of giving voice to the suggestion that we should honor those who lie in peace in the wastes of Siberia and Yakutsk.

* * *

---

[7] Ignalina, in the northeast part of Lithuania, is the largest nuclear reactor complex in the world. One of its reactors was similar to the infamous reactor in Chernobyl. On September 16-17, 1988, Ignalina was the scene of a 16,000-person demonstration which dramatized the Lithuanian nation's concern about the safety of this reactor complex. Shortly thereafter the third, nearly completed, reactor was closed, and the first reactor was shut down in 2005. The second is scheduled to be shut down in 2009.

[8] Vaižgantas (Juozas Tumas- Vaižgantas) (1869-1939), Lithuanian priest, writer, journalist, scholar, activist. Putinas (Vincas Mykolaitis-Putinas) (1893-1967), Lithuanian poet, playwright, novelist, literary historian and critic.

Sigitas Geda (b. 1943, d. 2008) was a Lithuanian poet who published over fifty books, a number of which have been translated into various other European languages. Sigitas Geda was also a member of the *Sąjūdis* Iniciative Group.

Geda's Address was translated from a transcription appearing in the August 10, 1988 issue of *Draugas*, a Lithuanian language daily newspaper published in Chicago, Illinois, which reprinted the speech from the official publication of the Lithuanian Restructuring Movement, *Sajūdžio Žinios* ("Movement News"). The re-establishment of Lithuania's independence was proclaimed on March 11, 1990, and Lithuania became a Member State of the European Union in 2004.

This translation was originally published in *Lituanus*, the Lithuanian Quarterly Journal of Arts and Sciences, Vol. 34, No. 4 (Winter 1989).

CLAN OF THE CENTAUR

Saulius Tomas Kondrotas

Translated by Tadas Klimas

This tale certainly creates a mood, one of mysticism, wonder, and ... fantasy, and it is likely that this story, published in Lithuania during the late Soviet period (albeit in essence for a restricted audience) likely is the very first Lithuanian story in the fantasy genre. It is also the first to set the fantasy in some ... fantastical version of Lithuania's past.

Something lies within us that causes us to draw in and creep about like a thief in the darkness of the night, or like a man who, dizzy with wine, greatly offends his master and then apprehensively awaits the morning to see how it all will end. From whence has this treacherous instinct come? I know this characteristic is not unique to me, for I remember how Kukovaitis, my father, would suddenly start awake from his seemingly peaceful noon-time siesta and would dart his gaze about as if looking for some foe lying in ambush. Back then, I did not know what the source of this fear was in my father: I thought perhaps he was really concerned for his life. But when I reached a mature age, I realized that the enemy forcing us to twitch awake and stare about resides within our very selves. But even further, I have now seen on several occations how my young son, Šventaragis, while playing, or practicing archery, or while deep in thought, will suddenly start and his muscles will jump, as if having received a shock. His pupils will be narrow and his body drawn tight like a lynx before a leap. All of us — including my father, and myself, and Šventaragis, are healthy and strong men, who should grab life by the horns and throw it on its side, who should make life kneel to us, who should make of life a useful tool to achieve our purposes with. But we are afflicted with a type of indolence, a certain indecisiveness of action and thought that makes us resemble a hand with its fingers outspread, through which life pours like sun-dried sand. Instead of ourselves ruling life, we allow ourselves to be ruled by it. We all of the time are waiting for something; however, judging from the way we act during this waiting, this something must be — disaster.

It seems to me someone of our family once made a mistake, and the results of this mistake have continued to persecute us. I even believe I know what kind of error it was. In a word, it seems to me the cause of our weakness must be searched for in the past.

Varšas told me the tale.

Varšas lay half-sitting on bear hides amongst a multitude of figures of men and animals carved from elm and juniper wood and smeared with grease mixed with ash. Many who have seen these figurines believe them to be tiny idols which he reveres and to which he prays silently when alone. But Varšas has explained to me that these are representations of those men and beasts whose lives he has taken over the course of his own unusually long existence. Still, I believe Varšas only told half the truth: his own life, in this way incarnating itself in so many different representations, has through the course of time become itself a holy thing to him. I think Varšas has deified his own life to such an extent that his real life appears to him not to be his own, but that of everyone. Listening on windy nights to the sounds of the forest, earth, air, and houses, Varšas imagines he has lived so long only because the lives of those he has killed have devolved to him.

It may be I am wrong, and the wooden figures are merely carved pieces of wood Varšas keeps to decorate his room, like a former hunter who decorates his home with the horns of elk and bison he has shot.

"Tell me, Varšas," I say to him, "Why have you decorated your room with those you have destroyed and not with those you have created?"

His white lips part just the thinnest amount into a smile; the ends of his fingers, thin with age, tremble.

"You'll find out when you reach my age, Utenis."

Varšas' voice is gentle and pleasant, and, after he speaks, the air in the room vibrates for a time. Varšas is dodging the question. But his answer is not really important to me. What is paramount is Varšas understands life. That is what I want to ask him about.

Varšas is my servant who does not serve. No, that is not quite correct. He performs no chores and brings me no flagons of water to drink; he does not prepare my bed and does not bring to it Princess Visgalė. He is too old for these things. But he serves us in other ways. Along the difficult road to awareness Varšas is our sole support. Varšas extends us a hand when we become tangled up in our thoughts, when we no longer know what to do, when we cannot think of how to punish the guilty, when, in sum, we want to know who, indeed, it is we are.

Varšas knows how to write letters. He served my father Kukovaitis; while yet a boy he served my grandfather Živinbudas. He has to know the answers to many questions that leave me no peace. He who knows how to write letters knows such secrets as people carry to their graves without having disclosed them to a living soul. There is no reason Varšas should hide anything from me.

He takes a strip of dried venison and begins to suck upon it, at the same time chewing it with his pale, soft gums. A small pile of dried meat lies before him on the table. Sucking on the meat, Varšas' eyes darken with pleasure, but their gaze is still riveted on me. It seems Varšas' glance holds it against me, that I am not as old.

The door is wide open. Outside the sun shines and wind blows. The north wind makes the trees dance and shake along with the bushes, the grass, and the few white clouds in the sky. The pure light of the sun is indifferent towards the earth. It is cold. I wrap myself tighter in my cloak, thinking of how best to explain to Varšas what it is I would like from him. Here, in the half-light Varšas' body seems light and transparent. At any moment Varšas could melt away like ice.

"Varšas," I say, "I want you to explain something to me."

He says nothing, merely gazing at the raging wind outside and at the swallows shooting across the fields. I could swear he knows the question I have come to ask him.

"How is it, Varšas, that we, living almost at the very center of our country, always feel as if we were at the ends of the earth? As if something were guarding us from the whole world, just like a gardener guards his vegetables."

Varšas shakes his head, not answering.

"No, Varšas," I say, "You know the answer. I command you. Give us the answer we are waiting for."

"You can order me or not, just as you please. At my age that signifies nothing."

"Answer me, Varšas." My tone suddenly loses its sharpness.

"People are happy when they are able to live quietly and without worry. It would be hard to imagine a life more peaceful than yours and your son's and your intimates'. You are fortunate. This whole world full of people boils and bubbles like a kettle of fat meat. It brims with danger, for people are predatory. You have no fear of such dangers, for no one has an eye to your domains or your life."

"Varšas, whatever I do, I always feel eyes fixed on me. I turn around swiftly, as unexpectedly as possible, but I see no one watching me. But, even so, there is someone watching me. They watched my father like that, and they are watching Šventaragis. We are all awaiting an attack. What is going on, Varšas? You know the answer."

"I know," quietly says Varšas. "I know."

A swallow flies into the room, circles around our heads, squawks, and flies outside again. There are many of those birds in this area, but right now I am excited and the swallow's flight into the room seems to me to be a sign with which to shut Varšas' mouth, to stop him from saying anything. A half-sigh, half-moan forces itself from me. My emotions are stretched to the limit. But Varšas does not see any of that. Now he, having fixed his eyes on one point, is searching for words with which to begin to speak.

So, like I say, Varšas told me the tale.

"The Centaur is to blame for everything," he said. "And Jučas, Jeremferden's servant, too. That was long ago."

Varšas' voice waxed stronger and then weaker, as if he were singing a long, slow hymn.

"But even longer ago, Mandazig's son Attila appeared; he, who, for his cruel nature, was named the Scourge of God. He murdered his three brothers — Achiar, Rocha, and Bledon — and the princess of a far land with eleven thousand of her handmaids who had sinned against no one. He liked thick, flowing blood. He enjoyed the color red, and his nostrils trembled like a wolf's at the pungent scent of warm blood. Having murdered his brothers, Attila reigned by himself in Hungary. With five hundred men of his clan, also thirsty for blood, he went to Italy, and everything living ran from him to hide in the cracks of the earth. Marcus Antonius Palemon, the son of the king of Pontus, became afraid of the word spreading about Attila and, with four clans of patricians, took flight in ships. After many long wanderings in oceans and seas, they reached the river Nemunas and sailed upstream, looking for a place where they could stop and live without fear, for they were ever haunted with a vision of Attila breathing down their necks. Sailing up the Nemunas, they came to the river Dubysa, turning up which they found high hills on either side, and, beyond those hills, wide meadows and luxuriant oak forests, full of game — bison, aurochs, elk, stag, deer, lynx, marten, fox, squirrel, ermine, and all sorts of others while the river teemed with unusual fish, and not only those which bred locally, but also many which came in from the sea, as the mouth of the Nemunas was not far.

Near these rivers, the Nemunas and the Dubysa, and near the sea, they settled and multiplied. They called that land Zemaitija.

The four clans of patricians who arrived here together were these: the totems of the Centaur, the Pillars, the Bear, and the Rose. Their leaders were Dausprung, Prospero Cezarine, Julian, and Hector. Palemon had three sons of whom only one, Kunas, had descendants: Kernius and Gimbutas. These also had a son apiece. To Kernius was born Živinbudas, and to Gimbutas, Mantvila. And when Živinbudas had as many years as now does your son Šventaragis, Prince Kernius took me from Bisenai at the age of eleven to serve him and his son Živinbudas.

"No, Varšas," I said to him, "My grandfather's name was not Kernius. You yourself said the Centaurs descended from Dausprung. You made a mistake, Varšas. That was so long ago."

"Attend me softly, prince. I have not erred. Your grandfather in truth was the brother of Mantvila Gimbutas-son. And you would to this day be the prince of the Palemons, if not for Jučas, may he not be reborn to a new life."

Varšas became silent, gathering his thoughts about the most important things, while I sat completely still and felt my face growing warm.

"Jučas was first seen by Sudvajus, Horsemaster for Prince Kernius, as Jučas, having swum the river, waded out from it and dried his clothes on the sun-heated sand of the riverfront. Jučas was a massive man. About thirty-five years of age, strong as a beast and with eyes of an indescribable color, eyes that pierced everything to and through. If of four jugs only one held milk, Jučas would reach right for that one, without even having lifted the cover to see what was inside. Jučas had one tremendous singularity: on his whole massive body, there was not a single hair. Not on his head, nor on his neck, nor under his arms, nor below his belly, like other men. He did not even have eyebrows, and his eyelids were without lashes. Jučas' sun-reddened skull was just exactly like the egg of a thrush. This all appeared very unusual, and we all would have wondered greatly at it, but Jučas bore himself as if not we should wonder at him, but that instead Jučas should wonder more at us. I would not, however, say that Jučas was haughty. For he could have presented himself as being a free man, and no one would have doubted it. But all the same he introduced himself as being a servant.

"I am Jučas, the servant of Jeremferdenas." Such were his first words, spoken to the prince. "Jeremferdenas sends his greetings."

The prince and his intimates did not know what to say in answer. No one had ever heard of Jeremferdenas.

"What do you want of us, Jučas? Who is Jeremferdenas?"

"My lord Jeremferdenas did not charge me to speak of him. He commanded me to bring you news that will sadden you. But Jeremferdenas does not wish you ill. Send for your brother, prince, and then I will impart to you what I have been charged with. And now let them show me where I can rest. For forty days and nights I have marched without sleep. I am fatigued."

Jučas' speech had been simple, without adornment, but impressive nonetheless. Immediately upon laying down on his bedding, Jučas fell asleep and did not rise until Prince Gimbutas rode in from Kaunas and the steel shod hooves of his horse sounded in the courtyard. Jučas had slept for four full days, not waking to eat, nor even having moved. I had brought food to him several times, but had always found him in the same position. It was also astonishing that Jučas slept with eyes wide open. When I would walk about in his room, the pupils of Jučas' eyes would follow my movements. But he himself truly slept. His breathing was regular, his body relaxed, the tip of his tongue hung out of his mouth, and from the corner of his mouth a trickle of saliva had run and dried.

Having come to the guest hall, Jučas bowed to both the princes and sat before them. We all waited for what he would say.

"Jeremferdenas sends his greetings to the house of Palemon," Jučas began, "And informs you, through his servant Jučas, that the House of Palemon is fated to perish in its twelfth generation."

I saw Prince Gimbutas' face grow pale and his hand squeeze the handle of his dagger, but Jučas did not even flinch.

"The men of the House of Palemon will kill each other or will simply pass away without heirs. Jeremferdenas, for whom there are no secrets in this land, has seen how the last of the Palemons dies with a flagon of wine in his hand. This my master has commanded me to say to you."

Jučas became silent, and all those who were there looked from one to the other in great confusion, angry or afraid. The first to recover from his astonishment was Prince Gimbutas.

"He is a trickster. Bind him."

But Prince Kernius stopped the servants.

"What house will arise after us?" he asked.

"The Clan of the Centaur," without cavil answered Jučas.

"And after them?"

"I do not know," said Jučas. "But Jeremferdenas certainly knows."

"Where is this Jeremferdenas?" growled Prince Gimbutas. "Show me his dominions. I will kill him."

"Jeremferdenas cannot be killed," calmly replied Jučas; it seemed he was immune to all passion, so well was he controlled. "You should not concern yourselves with him. At this time you should look to yourselves."

"If what you say is true, it hardly seems there is anything to be done," remarked Prince Kernius.

"But yet there is," answered Jučas. "One branch of your clan must become Centaur."

His words could have had just one meaning. In the region of Ukmergė there lived the sole descendant of Dausprungas. He would be condemned the moment one of the two princes sitting in the hall would agree to take the totem of the Centaur for his own.

For some time silence reigned in the hall. Again Gimbutas was the first to interrupt it.

"I don't believe a single word this beardless trickster has said."

He jumped up and stomped the ground from anger.

"Our house is eternal. No one can doubt that without fearing for their lives. I will slay the Centaur, and he will no longer threaten us, the Palemons, neither now, nor ever in the future. This l, Gimbutas, do swear."

"After the Palemons will come the Centaur," repeated Jučas, the servant of Jeremferdenas.

Prince Kernius kept his gaze fixed on Jučas' eyes. Prince Gimbutas trembled when he heard his brother say:

"I agree. Yes, I believe you, foreigner. My son Živinbudas will become the Centaur."

Prince Gimbutas, clenching his fists, exited the hall with his escort. We soon heard them riding away.

"From now you will have simply to wait," said Jučas. "You will do nothing more as you watch how, one after the other, your relatives will die. Your lives will be long and slow, but your relations' lives will be short, fiery, and without peace. Every step they take will bring them closer to the abyss, and every step of your own will bring you closer to that greatness which is fated for you."

"I agree," breathlessly repeated Kernius.

"But this is not all," Jučas said, rising and approaching Kernius to bend and whisper at his ear, so softly we could barely hear him. "This is not yet all. For the lives and honor of your clan you will have to pay."

Prince Kernius started, then leaned back and ran his gaze over Jučas from head to foot.

"No, not to me," Jučas almost smiled. "Neither Jeremferdenas or I need anything from you, you need have no dread of that. But, you realize, this is a matter of cheating the gods. You are deceiving them, not wanting to accept the fate which has been ascribed to you from there," he said, pointing up above. "That is a transgression, and transgressors are punished, are they not?"

"What type of punishment can we expect? Has Jeremferdenas not seen this?"

"No, he does not know this. But I myself greatly dislike the Centaur. Half man, half animal."

"But that is just a totem," weakly answered the prince.

"True," confirmed Jučas. "But so much is clear: this is the only way the House of Palemon can survive."

"But perhaps ..." Now the prince was beginning to feel uncertain. "Will we not be forced to pay too high a price for this?" he said, turning to us, as if seeking our support.

"Father,'" said Živinbudas. "I assent to being the Centaur." Jučas came to his full height and, for the first time during the days he spent with us, he laughed, showing strong, white teeth. Without uttering a further word he departed from the hall. After four or five days he, still without uttering a word, disappeared, never to be seen again.

Varšas became silent and fixed his gaze upon something behind me. I turned around. In the doorway stood Šventaragis, my son. His face showed he had heard Varšas' tale. In the beginning anger possessed me and I was about to throw something at him. But Varšas restrained me with a glance. Well, then, all to the better. Sooner or later Šventaragis would have to learn everything; he undoubtedly would eventually mature to those questions, just as I had.

"How much longer do we have to wait, Varšas?" he asked.

"Not long, lord," answered Varšas. "You are the fourth generation after Prince Kernius. But from Gimbutas there have

63

been already nine. Like Jučas said, they hurry to live and to die. Mantvila, Gimbutas' son, begot two sons: Vykintas and Erdvila. Vykintas died without heirs. Erdvila begot Mingaila. Mingaila begot two sons: Skirmantas and Ginvilas. Ginvilas begot Borisas, Borisas — Rogvolodas, Rogvolodas — Glebas, who died without heirs. Skirmantas begot Prisimantas, Liubartas, and Treniota. The first two died without progeny. Treniota begot Algimantas, Algimantas — his son Ringaudas. Ringaudas begot two sons: Mindaugas and Dausprungas. The latter begot Tautvila, who died having left no one. Mindaugas begot Vaišvilkas, Repeikis, Girstutis, and Rūklys. Of those four only Vaišvilkas remains, the ruler of Lithuania. He has no sons, no authority among the princes and nobility, has no virtue, and is completely given up to drunkeness. After him, Šventaragis, it is your turn, if Jučas was telling the truth."

"Leave us now, Šventaragis," I said, and he left looking so serious and thoughtful that it touched my heart.

"Are you happy with what you have learned?" asked Varšas when we were alone.

"I can say this, Varšas. I do not understand why that feeling of waiting which afflicts me is so much like a feeling of awaiting *disaster*. Should it not be the reverse?"

"You have become used to waiting without knowing for what. A person's life is arranged similarly to the four seasons. Joy's analog would be summer. The remaining seasons are cold, foul, wet, and grim. So much for man's dismal emotions," replied Varsss, and I perceived he knew nothing more and could be of no further help to me.

Again he took a piece of dried meat and began to gum it. The face of old age is repulsive, I reflected, as I left him and strode back into the day, which was brimful of sun and cold wind. Nearly four months of the usual waiting had past since that day until that happened, which, it appears, had to happen, and which has changed my view of the world and of the nature of man in its essence. Not even Varšas could give me any advice. He just sat, all enwrapped in ermine furs, looking with watery eyes at the reflections on the walls cast by the fire, and kept repeating:

"Jučas is the one who did all this. I know: Jučas is to blame for it all."

But in truth Jučas, who must long ago have become dust, was innocent of this charge. Nevertheless, Varšas could not give up and show he was incapable of giving some answer. What would his long life have been worth if it had become clear there were things he was powerless to understand? I did not gainsay Varšas, but it pained me to witness his pain and his own tormenting of his defenseless, impotent memory.

When the first snow came, when animals first begin to leave clear tracks that enable day-long pursuit, we held a wonderful, large hunt. Having invited guests from the neighboring areas, we planned to enjoy this diversion to the limit. The beasts were fat, having foraged through the cool summer and the long, warm fall; the fresh, squeaking snow reinvigorated their senses, like the touching of a newly closed wound, and they were yet quick and strong. How all of this — the crunching of the snow, the warm smell of the horses, the rough jests of the men, the fever of the hunt, the baying of the hounds, the sweat on the face from the effort of the riding and the throwing of the spear, the cup of yet hot, sweet blood from the neck of a freshly slain beast that caresses the parched palate and causes a feeling of unsurpassed satiety — how all of this renews a man's soul and forces the heart to beat at a faster rate!

Having broken all four spears I had taken with me, I, instead of sending a servant, turned my charger around and, heated by the passions of the hunt, galloped towards home. My falcon's name is Nestan. Varšas raised him for me, and he always accompanied me on the hunt. Nestan, unlike other falcons, did not need to have his eyes hooded while being brought to the place of the hunt or returned from there. As I would ride out, I would command that Nestan be released, and he would continually circle in the sky, high overhead, my silent companion. When the urge struck him, he would descend from the sky to rest upon my shoulder. But this occurred relatively rarely. Most often, I would lift my eyes skyward to see him, with his wings widely outspread, gliding high above in the sky.

The winter before last, while in the hunt, I had fallen from my mount and had injured my knee. I laid half the day in the already deep snow, unable to rise and remount my horse. The cold began slowly to seep into my body, and I began to think I would die, but then they finally found me. The lodestar of their search had been Nestan, patiently and loyally circling in the air over that area where misfortune had struck me. Anyone, wanting to know which side of the forest I might be on, needed only glance at the sky to gratify his wish.

I had spurred my mount and headed homeward, when suddenly I felt someone grip my shoulder strongly. It was Nestan, my falcon. His sharp talons pierced my clothing and painfully bit into my skin. I shook myself, wanting to throw off the bird and force him to fly. Nestanas eased his grip somewhat, but did not arise into the air. At another time I would have understood that Nestan wanted, in his own language, to tell me something, to communicate something to me, to affect my actions in some way. But at that time, like I said, I was excited and paid no more attention to the falcon. Nonetheless, when I think of it now, it might have been much better if he had continued to fly high overhead. Perhaps then everyone would have known where I was, and it would have been possible to avoid that which was to occur.

Jumping from my mount in the courtyard, I ran inside and hurried to my sleeping rooms, where I kept my spears, so that they would always be ready to hand if needed. Balčiukė, my wife's Princess Visgalė's, servant, upon seeing me became afraid and dropped an urn filled with ashes. But I paid no attention to this. With several strides I ran into the room and grabbed up a spear. I turned around wanting to speed back to the hunt. And then I witnessed a sight which I absolutely had not expected. In our wide bed, amongst long-wooled blankets, were lying two people: a man and a woman. Not wishing this and knowing nothing, as the God is my witness, I came upon them in that moment, when the passion of love and propagation had plunged them into oblivion. The white face of the woman, with eyes closed and hair spilling over the pillow, was that of my wife, Visgalė — and I had never seen her more beautiful. Who the man was I could not yet tell at that first glance.

My hand acted faster than thought. Giving off a short cry, as I was accustomed to doing in the hunt, as if to lend the arm additional strength, I drew back and let fly the spear with all my might. The well-made spear pierced the man to and through, for when he groaned and collapsed and then fell to the side, I could see that the point of the spear, coming out the far side, had left a small wound on Visgalė's breast.

Now I recognized the man. It was Lisica, one of our servants, a youngster of twenty years, whose glance and mouth for some unknown reason had always been full of derision. Because of that expression, he had always appeared wiser than in truth he was. I am convinced death found him before he had recovered from the intoxication of love-making, and that he had had no chance to return from the void. Blood coursed from his wound like water over ice when it is newly broken through; it poured out over Visgalė's stomach and thighs. She opened her eyes and stared at me, but she still did not see me. I thought she would begin to shriek and scream like all women. But when her gaze fixed on her lover and returned to me, I heard nothing. She did not move, did not even pull up the cover to hide her nakedness. Nevertheless, her eyes keenly followed me when I took into my hands another spear.

"You will follow him," I heard myself saying.

It was then she opened her lips to speak.

"We would not be born, if there were no other existence to wait for."

My face twisted, but in my heart I hesitated. Visgalė was an intelligent woman, very intelligent, and I have not to the present day ceased to wonder what impelled her into such a perilous path of secret love. I perceived, however, that her words were too wise for the occasion and were, therefore, false. Yes, there was uncertainty in her voice. As if she were assaying with a staff whether an abyss was to open up before her in that spot where she purposed to step. I never have understood women. They are too foreign. They live among us, and yet apart: like cats, who never attach themselves to a person. I never troubled myself overmuch with this, but even my mother, who loved me a great deal, was alien to me. Women are strange even just for their contention that they understand us, their sons, husbands, and brothers.

"Why did you do this?" I asked.

"Don't think this is the first time. I have been doing it all along."

Only now did she begin to recover. She began to shake and ceased holding herself in. She virtually went mad with anger. I stood there with a spear in my hand and a falcon on my shoulder and listened to her insulting words. The more impassioned she became, the calmer I grew. She spoke with pale lips.

"Nothing ever mattered to you other than that damned fate of yours. What kind of a man are you? Other men walk firmly upon the earth; they eat, drink, hunt, war, and do not forget to give their due to women. They are hale and do not concern themselves with nothings. What of it if you are taller and stronger than others if you only stare off into shadows, murmur nothings beneath your breath, and walk about as if in a dream. I even envied the maids that the man servants at least occasionally would lean them up against the wall in a dark corner. You never really needed me, and if you did, it was just to breed another demented half-prince like you. The Centaur! Just think. Half man, half horse. A full horse would be better. Don't you know everyone makes fun of your totem's other half — that it's no horse but a mare!"

I shook when she mentioned Šventaragis. All the rest of her jabbering was nothing and I knew it. Even she, if not for her anger, probably would not have spoken in this way. Nevertheless, I was greatly displeased by her belittling of Šventaragis. I trembled and raised the lance. The dark glistening eyes of Visgalė grew large.

"No!" she screamed. "No! You can't kill me! You don't dare!"

I answered nothing but merely brought back my spear, as if about to use it.

"I am the princess!" She was shrieking now. "I am your wife, do you hear? Don't you dare! I will call the servants. Yah! Help! No, Utenis, you won't dare."

She turned over onto her stomach and tried to crawl to me. Tears flowed down her cheeks, and her screams became hisses.

"You don't dare, you won't dare. You can't kill me, Utenis. You can't."

"I can," I said. "You very well know I can. You know even more: that I am going to. And no one in the whole world will stop me."

"No," Visgalė whispered, crawling closer. "No, no."

I drew back my lance, but then she lifted her head to me and that which I saw withheld my hand. Her dark and moist eyes became round and yellow like two translucent stones. Those eyes met my gaze without any emotion. I will never forget this. Somewhere I had seen eyes like unto those before, but at that time I could not recall where. I closed my eyes, and then it became clear. Such are the eyes of a viper. The short time I had my eyes closed was enough for me not to see the most important thing. When I looked again upon my wife, Visgalė, I no longer beheld the princess. In front of me on four crooked legs stood a large, man sized lizard, with protruding yellow eyes, a scaled hide, and a red maw, full of sharp teeth. Its throat pulsed. I froze, and the lizard stepped towards me. I drew away backwards and again brought back the lance. The lizard hissed and jumped towards the wall. I turned, intending to run out, and in the doorway I saw Varšas. He held me back with a gesture and pointed to Lisica, lying in the middle of the room. I gripped the end of the lance, lifted the run-through body and, so carrying it, walked out. Varšas slammed the door shut and barred it. When I turned to him, wanting to ask what, in his opinion, should be done next, I perceived that his whole body — his legs, thin as arrows, and his arms, carved with black, pulsating, finger-width veins, like snakes, and his decrepit throat with its sharp Adam's apple, and his large head with its closed eyes — was trembling and twitching. Having thrown down the lance with its speared corpse, I grasped the shoulders of the servant.

"Varšas," I said. "Calm yourself. Don't be afraid, Varšai." He continued to tremble like a frost-bitten boy. I don't quite remember what I myself was feeling. As if nothing.

I wanted to take care of everything before the end of the hunt. I had a good half-day's time.

We buried Lisica, chopping a hole in the frozen earth a league from the house. The biggest worry was the lizard. In the beginning I could not bring myself to think about it, that I would have to unbar the door of my sleeping chamber and go inside. But the reptile could not remain in the house. That we well understood, both I and Varšas.

"I would help you, but I am now too old and would just get in the way."

I heard sounds of the hunt carried by the wind, cries free and jubilant, the sharp baying of the hounds. Even when you go up against a bear with a knife, you are certain you will prevail. Otherwise you would not go. But now I was face to face with a phenomenon I could not comprehend, something completely alien. Therefore I did not even feel my strengths and options. As if I were suspended in the air, unable to gain purchase against the earth. Tears came into my eyes when I thought of how happy I had been just several hours ago. I wanted to still be in the hunt, I wanted that nothing should have happened.

"Take a strong and sharp spear." said Varšas. "No matter how sharp his teeth are, he will not withstand a weapon. Or perhaps it would be better to make a small hole in the roof and shoot through the hole with a bow until it dies?"

"No," I shook my head. "I cannot."

Because Varšas did not understand, I explained:

"I cannot go in and kill it in cold blood. One way or the other, that is Visgalė." It was hard for me to say these words; the abominable, dumb beast in no way comported with the image of my beautiful, intelligent wife which continued to stand before my eyes. Still, the words I had spoken were true.

"But at first you wanted to take her life. Now, when she has lost her form it will be easier for you to do so."

"I cannot," I repeated. "Do not try to persuade me, Varšas. I will not be able to convince myself. Before, my sinews acted without reference to my head. Now my head is once again in charge."

"Then everything is somewhat more complicated," Varšas said, deep in thought. "I no longer know how to help you. I will go be by myself for a time and consider."

I did not want to be left alone. I had no dark corner with figurines amongst which I could recover my balance. So I asked him:

"Stay here, Varšas. Right now I need you very much."

He agreed without a word.

In a short time we came to several conclusions. I had a cellar dug into a hill. It was a large, cold room with a door made of thick logs, split down the middle. If some one of us died during the summer, we would put their body in there, and it would not spoil for twenty or more days until the burial was prepared for in the appropriate manner. We decided to put the reptile in that cellar. The hardest problem was how to lead him from the house to the hill. But we found a solution.

Taking a rope as thick as a wrist, we made nooses in both ends. At the door we tied a horse and fixed one end of the rope to it. (Other than Balčiukė, there had remained in the house about ten people. I ordered them all to gather in one chamber, and, when all were inside, I locked them in for a time. I did not want what I wished to do in secret to be compromised by the household servants. The thus imprisoned did not even show much displeasure: apparently, I looked very wroth and, of course, they could clearly see my clothes, covered with Lisica's blood.)

And so, more calm now we were certain of not being discovered, we continued our design. Varšas carried my lance. He held it with both hands, firmly clenched, but even so he was hard put to retain his hold: his weakened fingers kept opening; his face from the strain was flushed with some kind of old, dark, yet somehow grey, reddening; the wrinkles in the corners of his eyes and mouth vibrated; the widely stepping feet barely upheld his body, weighed down by his burden. But Varšas bore it heroically. What impelled him? Devotion? Habit? Self-respect? Stubbornness? The conviction that without him I would fail? I do not know. I carried the noose. I shot the bolt open and abruptly jerked the door open. My heart pounded, expecting an attack. But the reptile did not attack. It lay in the same place where we had last seen it, stretched out in its full length, with its head lying on the floor. One of its eyes, yellow, cold, and sparkling, regarded us without moving.

It had to be made to move: as long as the lizard's head stayed on the ground, it could not be ensnared in the noose. I took the spear from Varšas and stepped closer, suddenly calm and no longer worried, as if I had been catching such creatures all my life. Women transformed into lizards. I made no unnecessary or clumsy moves. Holding out the lance, I tapped the animal with the sharp end in the neck: even with a spear it was unpleasant to come near it. It lifted its head and angrily opened its maw. In that instant I threw the noose. It was not even necessary to make the horse, standing outside, move in order to tighten the rope, so swiftly did the lizard jump to the other side of the chamber and toss about until the noose was tight and it began to choke. Our fears proved unwarranted, for it did not act like a human being, but like any animal. Instead of having jumped to our side so that the rope would loosen, it panicked and tried to run from us, in this way itself helping us achieve our goal.

Varšas was now just as calm as I.

"Along with her body, God took away her mind," he said. "Poor thing."

A lump arose in my throat, but I swallowed it down.

"Take the horse towards the hill, Varšas," I commanded him. "I will walk alongside with the spear and make sure nothing happens."

Soon the sturdy doors of the hill-cellar swung shut in order to trustily safeguard the strange creature. Varšas was breathing hard but smiling. I heard in the distance the voices of the returning hunters and hurried to release the servants and domestics.

In the evening, forcing myself to smile and urging the revelers to make merry, I felt sorrow and longing. Like never before I longed for my beautiful Visgalė, beloved wife. I would have given anything to find her at my side. Seeing that the men had grown intoxicated, I rose and left the hall unnoticed. Snow fell silently in large clumps; a dog yelped from choking on a bone or from an injury to his side sustained in the hunt. Other hounds, having left him alone, with eager, damp snouts milled about among the guests or ate cooked meat, of which there was abundance. For a time I listened to the lone dog's whimpers, then, wading through the snow, I went to visit Varšas. He was sitting near the fire, watching the flame with glistening eyes. He did not turn at my entrance.

"Jučas is to blame for everything, the servant of Jeremferdenas . . . Not a single hair on his whole body ..."

I had thought to find solace with Varšas. Alas. I returned to the night and snow, which immediately covered my shoulders, hair, and beard. It melted when it fell upon my heated face. My body was full of never experienced feelings, as if I stood at the boundary of a completely other existence. Visgalė . . . How I needed her now! Feelings flowed in my heart, my chest; hard and chill like an icy fluid. I had never experienced anything like it. I stood with eyes closed under the naked sky. I longed for the past. The dog continued to whimper. It snowed.

After a time I realized I was no longer alone. Someone other than I had come outside. Deep in thought, I had not noticed. I saw a dark shadow several steps away. I could not tell if he could see me or not. Nevertheless, I could not stand there any longer, almost totally covered in snow. I shook myself to lose at least some of the snow and walked toward him. The man, shorter than myself, was standing with his back to me, with his head thrown back and turned upward to the heavens. The snow crunched under my feet, and he turned around slowly, as if displeased that someone was disturbing his interesting and important work.

"What are you doing here?" I asked.

"I knew you were here," he answered. "I saw you leaving the hall."

"What could you have need of from me at such a time, Šventaragis?" for, in truth, it was my son.

He did not reply at once, but remained silent. I was uneasy, fearful he would inquire of that upon which I wished to remain silent. The cold began to grip me. The night would be truly frigid. Šventaragis, it seemed, did not feel the cold. He again leaned back his head and, with his mouth wide open, tried to catch the falling snowflakes. He looked like an idiot.

"Well? Say something, Šventaragis."

He turned around, and from the light in his eyes I could tell he was intoxicated. He had had too much wine. From that time, when I had allowed him to participate in the hunts, Šventaragis had also participated in the banquets. Sometimes he would drink. I did not like that, but I gave him the benefit of the doubt. Even though of tender years, he was a person who perfectly understood his limitations and would not even dream of attempting something he could not achieve. That is a rare

75

quality. Even those come into their years of mature discretion tend to overrate themselves and their capacities.

"Since returning from the hunt, I have not seen my mother. Where is she?"

But I had been expecting that.

"She is at her sister's."

"Without saying goodbye to me ..."

"She was in a hurry." I thought such an answer would satisfy him, but I was wrong.

"Who escorted her?" Even intoxicated, Šventaragis did not lose the clarity of his mind.

"Lisica."

"Lisica?" I could feel in his voice great anger and bitterness.

"Lisica?" he repeated and was about to add something, but bit his tongue and remained silent.

I then comprehended he knew about poor Visgalė's relationship with the servant. It angered me that even my son knew more than I. Suddenly Šventaragis lifted up his head, and in his look I could see suspicion.

"Are you certain mother truly went to her sister's?"

"Yes."

I had answered too quickly and too strongly. Šventaragis at once understood I knew everything. Everything he, for who knew how long, had hidden from me.

"Why did she act like this?" His voice was at once both disappointed and insultingly sharp.

"It is improper to judge one's parents."

He squeezed the handle of his knife.

"I'll kill Lisica. I'll catch him and do him in. I'll find him no matter what!"

"That is no longer necessary."

He gave me a sober look; he understood.

"And mother? You said he escorted her."

"Almost ..."

"What happened to her? Where is she?"

"She is not here." The cold's grip was ever more chill, but my back was wet from sweat: I was not bearing this inquisition easily.

"You killed her?"

"No."

"I don't believe you."

"I swear to you," I said, feeling some relief in telling the truth.

"I thank you," said Šventaragis. "It would have been very unpleasant for me if you had soiled yourself with my mother's blood."

Although I was not wanting to speak, he raised his hand to ask my silence.

"Let's speak no more of this."

Suddenly I felt as I had felt many a time before, that someone was watching over my shoulder. Šventaragis also gave a start. When after a time he went back inside, I turned around. Directly behind me stood the *hill with the cellar.*

I can now swear with certainty that time disappears for that person whose senses are multiplied a thousand times and then are made a thousand times stronger. I began to understand those wise philosophers who abuse themselves with fasting and thirst in the dead of the forest so as to perceive the world as it really is, as it really is in itself, so as to experience the holy joy of touching with the tips of one's fingers that quintessent reality which has no top, nor bottom, nor beginning, nor end. I had not reached the levels of the masters, but I now could understand them. Having no other way to awaken their soul, they scourge their flesh.

Varšas was in any case smarter than I. If not for him, I would have died that winter. He fed me with concoctions of bees' honey, heated syrup, and milk; made me drink of many different herbs; ordered me to swallow spiders' webs folded into spheres the size of peas; and only because of him was I able to continue to be able to draw breath and to make some sense of the reality lofting me skyward (although in the deep, dark winter nights, full of delerium, I called it a reality casting me down). If not for Varšas, who himself was just barely hanging on because in truth he was already standing near the border of oblivion, I would have died one of those winter mornings while snowflakes were quietly falling and never would have realized that I was dead. But Varšas did not abandon me, and when snow began to melt from the rooftops, I became aware one day that I lay in my chambers, enwrapped in furs, among which I saw Varšas' white ermine.

During that time while I was elsewhere I learned much, although not everything. Most importantly, I forgave Visgalė her transgression. Now her form ceased to be important to me. No room was left in my consciousness for a reptile. I thought of my wife as of a woman, such as she once had been. I swore to myself I would not lose her. In my thinking I felt no repulsion toward that awful, unhappy creature her body had become.

I heard footsteps, and into my chambers ran Balčiukė, carrying two steaming clay pots. Meeting my gaze, she stopped. I smiled.

"How wonderful! How wonderful you have recovered, my prince!"

"Was I ill?" I asked.

The girl became confused, not knowing whether she could tell me all. After a moment she drew up her courage and said:

"I don't know. I've never seen anyone be sick like that. People were saying . . . But Varšas said this was an illness and that you definitely would recover. How wonderful!"

Through the window sunshine was slanting in, lighting up Balčiukė's face from one side and enhancing the beauty of her features. I felt how a light tremor ran down my spine, as if a breeze had blown by.

"Come closer, Balčiukė," I said.

She put her pots on the floor and approached trembling. At one moment I almost forgot myself and came near to saying, "Visgalė." It seemed to me everything that had happened from the day I had rushed home with Nestanas on my shoulder to get some spears was just a dream. But upon opening my eyes I saw Balčiukė's smooth eyelids, and the illusion vanished.

When everything was done and we rested for a time, I questioned Balčiukė as to whether there had been any changes in my absence. Nothing had happened at home, but in the world — much. Prince Levas during a banquet had killed King Vaišvilkas with a knive: Vaišvilkas, the last of the Palemons. I was shocked. What is this, coincidence, or the fulfillment of old prophesies? I wanted to get more detailed information. I turned to the girl:

"Get dressed and call Varšas to me. I want to see and speak with him."

She obeyed. Swiftly she threw on her dress and was on her way out when she remembered why she had come in. She placed near my bed vessels of food, which smelled of mint, thyme, and meat, and then hurried off to find Varšas.

"Glory be to the Creator of the world," said Varšas. He stood leaning on a thin rod of birch — which was enough to uphold that shadow of a body — and his eyes shone with joy, for it could well be said he had caused me to be born anew. At that moment he was father and mother to me. He approached and kissed my forehead.

Balčiukė had told the truth. Vaišvilkas was dead. But she had not known the whole story. The princes had deliberated and decided Šventaragis was the best candidate for the throne. They had sent a messenger to ask for my consent, but not able to obtain that, Šventaragis, having counselled with Varšas, made his decision independently. He ordered the messenger to report his consent to rule the country. There remained only his coronation ceremonies, which were to occur in several months. Jučas had not lied. I was the father of the ruler of Lithuania.

"You are not happy, prince," said Varšas.

"I am happy," I answered, "But I would be even happier if Visgalė, my princess, would be able to share my happiness."

"Alas," spoke Varšas with his head bowed low.

"How is she?" I asked weakly: I could not remember or speak of her without sorrow. "How is she?" I repeated.

"More probably a `he.' Although it is hard to tell anything about that lizard's gender."

"How is she," I repeated.

Varšas took my meaning and from then on also spoke of — her.

"All winter I fed her and cleaned the cellar as well as I was able. I did not know what food would be suitable. Now I can say raw meat is best for her. At the beginning she would not eat anything . . . she would take nothing and would stare at the door as if wanting to escape. But now everything is well."

"Could a miracle happen?"

"I do not know. My heart tells me it has already occurred, and you will never again witness her in the shape of a woman."

I was myself convinced of that, though I did still retain some hope.

"Were you not afraid, Varšas? You are not so able."

"When you . . . took ill, after a month I bought a tamed bear. She was afraid of the bear."

For some time we both remained silent. Then I spoke.

"Have you not changed your opinion, Varšas?"

"No. I still believe this to be retribution for a deception committed long ago. It is possible Jučas knew even then, but did not say."

I believed him easily, somehow of itself, as if in my head there had long been prepared a place for such a thought. One might even say I took some ease from it.

"There is no guarantee such a misfortune might not yet afflicts someone else as well. I do not believe it could happen to Šventaragis, but perhaps to someone else of the household. We all must be wary."

I remained silent, gazing at that spot where the sun had so recently illuminated Balčiukė. I wanted her anew.

"Thank you, Varšas," I said. "Now I will begin to look after things myself."

I never would have thought there would come to be a time in my life when a beast would become the most important being to me in the whole world. But this came to be. Two persons, who had been close to me all the time and even in a certain sense a part of me, slowly but surely began to draw away from me. The first of them, Varšas, who given up so much strength and effort in nursing and caring for me during the entire season of winter, grew weak. If he had not already been so ancient, the best words to describe his complete decrepitude would have been 'old age.' After the snow had melted, Varšas no longer went out from his peaceful room. He no longer had the strength. Although I did everything I knew how, it was clear Varšas would not see another winter. He just lay in a permanent twilight, became calm and at peace with everything, barely able to move his hands, while his eyes faded and faded until finally they completely lost their color, only just barely shining like two amethysts. To communicate with him was almost impossible. In order to hear what he was saying — more accurately, to hear what he was trying to say with his numb, withered mouth — one had to put one's ear to his lips. But even when he did hear, he did not always understand. Various times, past and present, grew so muddled in his mind that, having bent my ear to listen, I once received a promise from him that he would be a good boy and would never again wet his bed. In this way, gradually, a little at a time, I lost Varšas.

The other person whose nearness I missed, but did not have the courage to demand, was Šventaragis. He avoided me. When I would approach, he would remove himself at the first opportunity. I do not know what motivated him to act in this manner. He probably did not believe my oath that I had not killed Visgalė, his mother, and, his first flush of agitation having passed, he had begun to grieve and to long for her. I did not want to make, nor indeed could I have made, any explanation to him which would have restored his faith in me, so I believe he considered me the killer of his mother. He restricted himself to only those relations between us which were unavoidable. Varšas had told me that during the entire winter Šventaragis had not once entered the chambers in which I lay. It may be I was wrong and Šventaragis had simply needed to be by himself and to collect himself. He had to make ready from inside to become the sovereign. I would have given anything to have been able to see inside my son's heart. But that, of course, no one could give me.

Under these circumstances I became friends with an animal. That was Kutlubugas, the bear purchased by Varšas. Removed from the woods and from others like himself, he, it seems, also needed a creature with whom he could associate. During the first days after having taken him over from Varšas, I had kept and led him by a chain, because the bear seemed short-tempered and likely to attack me. But I soon saw his irritability was more likely a facade or, more accurately, that which I held to be irritability was his habitual attitude, demonstrating he is not slumberous, but is alert. When he would be full of meat and become lazy, he would stop growling, and would become sluggish and indifferent, as long as no one would bother him. Having discovered these features in him, I removed the chain, for Kutlubugas always perfectly walked at one's side, never trying to run or otherwise make any opposition. But I shortly had to replace the chain, because, having attached himself to me, the bear felt enmity towards the rest of the household. It required but a more harshly spoken word or a quicker motion to cause Kutlubugas, growling and with wide open jaws, to rise up on his hind legs, ready to attack. No one in the household could stand the bear, just as Kutlubugas disliked them. He had given his entire beastly soul up to me. Wherever I went or rode, I would take him along. Being left alone in the house, he would bellow and tear at the doors with his claws, driving great fear into the servants. The horses at first were afraid of the bear, but they soon grew accustomed to him and would greet him from afar with their neighing. Sometimes, having awakened in the night and not being able to fall again to sleep, I would listen to the chirping of the crickets in the dark, gently running my hand through Kutlubugas' fur and speaking with him: I would speak all sorts of nothings, as if a mother to her child or a man in love to his girl, or I might tell him of my life. The bear would growl contentedly, and then I would begin to question him regarding all sorts of matters, saying to him, "What do. you think about that, Kutlubugas?" Kutlubugas did not grow fond of Balčiukė, and I ceased to invite her: women no longer had any attraction for me. I would awaken in the early morning, when Kutlubugas, murmuring and sighing, would lick my feet. Then I would arise and take up some meat that had been laid aside the evening before, and would walk to the cellar hill. Yes, I would visit her every day.

Even having decided not to view her as a lizard, at first it was difficult. The unventilated cellar was full of some sort of strong, oppressive odor. I never found her asleep. The glassy gaze of yellow eyes would always meet me. I felt some sort of distress in my conscience. Although she was virtually in terror of Kutlubugas, I did not dare to enter without the bear. And the bear was entirely indifferent to her. I would throw the meat down on the stone floor and would immediately make my exit. She would not touch the meat in my presence. She would simply stare at me unceasingly all the while I was there. I tried to spend as little time there as possible. That duty depressed me.

With time, I slowly began to grow used to it. Already in a month I caught myself thinking that her eyes show she still has awareness. I would try to communicate with her, asking, when I would come in, "How are you, Visgalė?" But I never received any response. Not a word, not a gesture. But nevertheless my feeling did not weaken, although it was never reinforced. I was probably wrong, and my wish to see in her traces of humanity rendered me blind to my error. I became accustomed to speak with her in the same way I would chatter with the bear in the night. Even though the talk would be all one sided, having poured out my worries, apprehensions, and problems, having told her of what I was happy or of what I dreamt, I would feel better. A person after all must have someone to speak with. I came to understand that only after I began to converse with animals. Sometimes from the depths of my memories would arise some memory from the beginning of my life with Visgalė, from youth, or from childhood, and I, telling the story, would cry. But she, on her part, would make no response whatever to my remembrances or my tears. Kutlubugas would sometimes lick my tears away. He liked them for the salt.

More and more often I would think about the past. The further removed, the more real it became, and the more important for me. I loved the past's Visgalė as if in the present. With my whole heart I hated those, of whom I had sometimes felt unfavorably or whom I had belittled. Very close to me became my mother, whom in childhood I had poorly understood; I felt a deep respect for my father, whom I had formerly been afraid of. But Visgalė took up most of my thoughts. My memory reawakened even such details of our life which I had never noticed, or had noticed and immediately forgotten. As if before me I saw her as a shy maiden with upright breasts, disrobed for the nuptual bed; I saw her white, even teeth as she laughed at Šventaragis crawling on the furs; I reached out my hand, wanting to touch her, as she danced the sacred dance for Šventaragis to grow strong and hale. But the hand gripped only air, the eyes perceived, after a time, the wall or the table, and that, which had seemed to be laughter, was only the squeals of the young servant girls. Longing would grip my heart, and I would promise to think no more of this and to cease tormenting myself, but I would not hold true to my promise. Nor, in reality, was this in my power. Without noticing it, I would drift away into the past, realizing it only upon my return. In small stages I began to understand Varšas: what meaning his dried and soot-blackened figurines had held. I do not know how long this process of understanding would have taken until complete. But nothing is permanent. We must be wary, says Varšas. Something more must yet occur. And it did.

One morning I woke while it was yet dark, and although I had slept but little, I was in very good spirits, better than I had felt for some time. I rejoiced, without myself knowing why. I felt young and strong: I even tried to wrestle with Kutlubugas. Then, cheerful and excited, I fixed the chain to the bear and, taking some meat, went out to the hill. It may well have been such a night as lends energy to everyone (on such nights the best, strongest, and smartest children are conceived), because this time even *she* was not lying in the depths of the cellar, by the wall, but stood in the middle of the floor with her head up, as if listening to sounds coming from afar.

My head was a bit light from the strange joy, and, it appears, that was enough to give birth to an unwise thought. For the first time in many days I felt an urge to give delight to *her*. I fancied letting her out for a bit into freedom, so she could breathe fresh air and look, with eyes disused to the light, towards the heavens, which she had not seen for so long a time. I went out, leaving the door open, and tied the bear to a tree. I myself stood nearby, watching what would happen. After a time her unwieldy body crawled out from the dark of the cellar and froze in the doorway. For some time she stood motionless, breathing in the pure air through her round nostrils, and then she moved. If necessary, I thought, with Kutlubugas' help I would easily return her to the cellar. I felt good for having released her for this space.

Suddenly the bear bellowed. I turned around, but I was able to glimpse only the silhouette of a rider and hear the frenzied galloping of his mount. Šventaragis, with his thighs gripping the sides of the horse, with arm thrown back and spear ready to fly, was racing right at her.

"No!" I screamed, but was too late.

The blade of the spear pierced the side of the reptile and tore out a hunk of flesh. The lizard curled up from the blow into a shape like a crescent moon, and from its throat escaped a strange, gasping sound. Šventaragis forced the horse backwards, tore out the spear, and began to draw back for another attack. Quicker than I could myself believe, I ran up and, grasping the haft of the spear, pulled it towards me. He swayed and fell off the saddle. Immediately he let go of the spear, jumped up, and drew his sword. \ drew backward, with one eye on Kutlubugas, who was throwing himself forward against the chain ("Let him only not break loose!"), and the other on the young face, twisted with rage, full of terrible sorrow. Šventaragis drew back with his shortsword and struck — I felt a piercing agony in my stomach.

"Take that," he snarled. "Take that. For mother. You'll not fool me anymore."

I could hear his teeth grind, as if they were crushing stone.

"Šventaragis!" I did not understand, it never occurred to me I was seriously injured. "Calm yourself. I am your father. Your mother —"

He again drew back his sword and again struck, spitting out, "Take that."

Two more times I felt steel cut me to the quick: flames sprouted up in my body. I grasped my belly with my hands, and only then saw there was nothing there to hold together: I had no stomach. In its place was only a sticky mess of meat, pieces of cloth, and blood. My legs bent, and I crumbled to the ground. I saw how Šventaragis wiped his sword on the lower part of his robe, slipped it back in its sheath, turned around and jumped back onto his mount. I wanted to scream something out to him, but I could not. Not only because I was too weak. My entire body was gripped by a cramp. Fear. An indescribable, animal-like terror stole over me when I understood I was dying. I had never been so afraid. Nothing was left of me, but only fear. My body was that of terror. Everything, all my senses, all the pain, all merged together into one thing — fear. The orbs of my eyes hardened, my skin ripped and tore into a thousand shreds. I lifted my head and looked at Šventaragis galloping away into the distance. What I then perceived was the final blow. Something was different with the world. No, not with the world, but with me. I was different. *I had changed into a lizard.*

I was fated to die as a lizard. Suddenly my mind was clear. I understood everything completely. We were both wrong, both Varšas and I. Jučas was not at fault, as were neither the totem of the Centaur, fate, or the gods. Only just *fear* itself had transformed us into awful reptiles, animals, my wife Visgalė and me. Nothing other than it, this feeling, incongruent with man's birthright, but nevertheless overwhelming him, was the cause of all the evil that had happened to us. The fear of oblivion, of no longer being able to play with one's feelings and sensations, of losing everything. If we had given ourselves over in this way to happiness, we would simply have melted away into the thin air. But we were afraid. We were possessed by terror for our lives. Fear had *made us be like this.* Was it necessary to die in order to learn this? Oh, my poor dear Visgalė, my poor dear intelligent girl. How terribly she must have been afraid of me when . . .

I tried to rise, to get all four feet under me and crawl, but blood poured from me in waves and I was unable to move. Then I felt something presse itself to me. I turned my head and saw her. A lizard, such as me, with a gaping wound in her side, had crawled and lain down beside me, so that there was no space between us. A damp tongue licked my neck. We, Prince Utenis and his wife Visgalė, of the Clan of the Centaur; we, two people, man and wife, having experienced emotions of surpassing strength; we, two reptiles with amber colored eyes, died on dew-laden grass as the sun rose on a summer morning. That, which had separated us, now served to bring us together. Be happy, my son.

* * *

Saulius Tomas Kondrotas (b. 1953 Lithuania) requested political asylum in the West in 1986. He worked for a time for Radio Free Europe in Germany. This story (orig. title: *Kentauro herbo giminė*) is from a collection of his short works (also) entitled *Kentauro herbo giminė* (Periodika 1989). This translation was published in *Lituanus*, the Lithuanian Quarterly Journal of Arts and Sciences (Vol. 34, No. 2 Summer 1988).

From a review by Justinas Žilinskas. 'If truth be told, the first time I took Kondratas' short stories into my hand, I realized that nothing similar had ever been published in the Lithuanian language: some sort of strangeness, inexplication, irrationality, mysticism and even elements of fantasy. ... Without a doubt, such a writer could not be very well [officially] received or published in large printings for the public, which was so wrapped up in studying the details of the socialist existence [trans. note: this is meant sarcastically] ... especially after he emigrated to the West in 1986. [The reviewer mentions that several of Kondratas' other works had wound up in so-called 'special funds,' meaning that they were available in libraries only to those with special permission.]

Regarding [the short story Clan of the Centaur] – this has to be one of the first Lithuanian stories written in the fantasy genre. It is a strange tale, a purported history set back in Lithuania's pagan past, about a clan which is afflicted by a most unusual curse ... Without a doubt, in many of these stories the plot is not the most important feature (sometimes there just plain isn't one), but the mood and the details are what is important, which create the atmosphere of unreality and fantasy ... .'[1]

1 Justinas Žilinskas, Senoji Skaitykla, *[Review] Saulius Tomas Kondrotas: Kentauro Herbo Giminė* (Mar. 1, 2001) http://senoji.skaityta.lt/boardbin/article.cgi?page=KentauroGimine. (Quoted material translated by Tadas Klimas.).

FLAX BLOSSOMS

Vincas Ramonas

Translated by Tadas Klimas

We dwell in cities and take our summers and times outdoors in carefully measured fragments. There used to be some who did not and their feelings and passions could ripen over time, the way, perhaps, it should be.
The rest of us have this short story.

It was high summer. The earth was ripe, the wind a haze, laden and redolent with the golden, intoxicating dust of flowers. Wild poppies and bluebells were blooming. Blue flax also stood in bloom.

On a morning like this, she herself was like a raspberry, full of summer and longing. Her eyes sparkled strikingly, as if she had stood for a long time next to a hot flame. Her blouse was unbuttoned at the top so that the wind could caress her white throat. That's why — to pick red poppies to complement her dark hair — she waded far into the rye.

Her father was angered, "There's no dissuading her! What's come over her? She'll only trample the rye."

With the maple rake over her shoulder she walked past the blooming flax. On her eyebrows formed tiny, fragrant drops of dew. Her eyes were partly closed from a sleepless night. Sleepless because all night the caraway had emitted their scent; sleepless because all the moonlit night the village dogs had barked. Far, far away lightning had flashed, and it had been dreadfully hot in the granary under her downy covers.

Because it was summer, because everything was succulent, because everything blossomed and flamed.

In the meadow by the linden she saw their young hired hand. He was in his shirtsleeves, cutting the grass. His sleeves were rolled up and his chest was tanned where the unbuttoned shirt revealed it. His dark hair was tousled by the wind. Today she really found him handsome, somehow. After the sleepless night. Those strong arms, that chest and that dark hair, strewn across his forehead.

"May the Lord aid you! Well, have you gathered enough hair-grass?"

"Thank you. Enough for us both to bed down with."

The young man slowly leaned on his scythe and examined her from head to toe. Especially long did he mark her blouse.

The young man's glance and words strangely irked her. As if someone had softly caressed that concavity at the base of her throat. She grinned somehow strangely, looked him in the eyes and then, as if in defense, threw a handful of flax blossoms at his face. Right into his hair. Right into those eyes, so hotly and stubbornly staring. Darkly green. Dear.

He blinked his eyes shut. And his first impression, when he opened his eyes again, was that her blouse would just tear open. So thin and tight it was.

She slowly turned, smiling, and walked off. A red wild poppy blossom burned in her dark hair.

In the meadow she filled her wooden sandals with water. Stopping, she poured the water out of them and glanced back.

"Sandals! These were sandals once. Too small, worn out. If you were nice, you'd make me some new ones," she peeved him with her eyes partly closed. "And now — you only lie around at noon under the linden and sing the same tune all the time, always that "We will drive the grey oxen into the green forest." Oh, you and your oxen!"

He was still leaning on the scythe. Its end sank deeper and deeper into the earth.

"Well, cut then! Why are you staring with your mouth open?"

As if coming awake, he started slowly to whet the blade of his scythe, making it ring, without taking his eyes from her. Suddenly he gave a start, threw the scythe on the grass and biting his teeth grasped a finger of his right hand.

"Did you cut yourself?"

He was silent. Carefully he wiped the cut with grass.

She came nearer, looked at the blood, then at his eyes, and as if fearful she turned away. Suddenly she tore a strip of her thin blouse from her breast and turned back to him.

"What are you doing?"

"Give it here," she answered, breathlessly.

She took his hand, suddenly brought it to her lips and sucked away the running blood, looking him in the face with eyes of dreamy reverie. Then she quickly, with trembling hands, bandaged the wound, pushed back his hand, and walked away without looking back.

The young man, following her with his eyes, picked up the scythe from the meadow and began mowing with a stubborn concentration. He cut the mounds and the rocks. The red blood kept oozing through the fabric of her blouse onto the maplewood handle of the scythe.

* * *

Around noon near the woodshed he was carving soles for a pair of wooden sandals. From willow. Very light. For some very pretty sandals. He wanted to make the sandals so pretty, so pretty . . .

Seeing her going towards the granary, he placed the axe on the wood-chips and asked,

"Will they be all right?"

"What 'all right'?"

"The soles for the sandals. You could try them for size."

She stood for a moment as if uncertain. Then she came close and, without saying a word, put her foot on the new sole. He took her foot and could in no way place it correctly. His hands trembled. The whiteness of her feet, their roundness, and the warmth . . .

"Well, as if you know how to measure! And the soles are too big." She was not pleased.

"So, I can't even make sandals? This is the first time in my life I hear this!" Placing the soles on the stump used to chop wood, he chopped them in half with two blows of his axe, threw everything to the ground and quickly walked away through the yard.

He fell under the linden onto thick grass and looked up somewhere, at the green leaves, at the blue sky. The linden tree rustled so green, so blue, unboundedly so. He felt somehow sad, even angry. To the point where something hurt in his chest.

* * *

The night was unusually close. One's hands sweat, one's feet were hot. In the hay recently brought from the meadows to the hay barn. The sleepy gnats buzzed and kept sleep away.

Outside heavy dew was on the grass. Deep summer peace. The lindentree's flowers were fragrant in the moonlight. Caraway and red apples gave off their fragrance in the orchard near the granary. Near the window of the granary.

Far away the north was pink.

And there was this mysterious temptation. In the closeness of the fragrant summer's night. There was something of a pull — to the granary window. And that path to the granary was just too easily descried this night. It was like torture. Like a temptation.

Having gazed for a long time through the crack in the boards, he arose. Too sticky, too close. No sleep to be had anyway. He stepped out into the yard, and the night's coolness caressed his hands swollen from the heat. He walked along the path to the granary; he then stopped, and

thought, and shook the orchard fence: a little, but as if he wanted to tear it down.

Those flax blossoms she had thrown at him had struck him straight in the heart. Straight in his blood.

Having taken off his shoes he carefully approached the granary and knocked on the window.

"Are you asleep?" He could barely talk.

Silence.

"Anelė, are you asleep?"

An apron covered the window. The apron parted, and Anelé appeared silently looking out through the glass.

"Open it. I want to tell you . . ."

"You, apparently, have lost your mind."

"Open it, Anelé . . ."

"No. I can't. But what, after all, is the matter with you?"

A pause.

"See, what you're like . . . And why did you throw those blossoms at me? No, I won't forgive you . . ." With a firm blow of his fist he broke the windowglass and tried to grab her hand.

"Anelé . . ." He was hardly able to breathe.

But she managed to step away.

Grabbing her apron he tore it from the window and squeezed it in his hands. He gritted his teeth and suddenly ripped the apron in half. Then he threw it back through the broken window, and walked back along the path. He found his shoes, shook the sand out of them, and put them on. Without being really aware of what he was doing he went into the horse stables. He even threw some clover into the feeding troughs. Softly he patted the horse's neck.

"Eat, eat. Ah, well, go ahead, eat, Blackie . . . Ah, just you wait!"

* * *

The next morning they both drove to bring in the dry clover into the hay barn. Having climbed into the wagon she kept looking at him all the time, she kept smiling fleetingly while he drove. He turned unexpectedly and saw that smile. But it was a clear teasing. She was feeling great as a woman and she was teasing him.

He sharply cracked the whip at the horses and energetically pulled at the reins. The horses reared. Such was her smile.

Loading the wagon he speared the clover with his pitchfork and lifted up almost an entire stack. He just about blanketed her in clover. As if he wanted to cover that strange smile of hers. But her smile continued to irk him from under the meadow-flowers and the dry clover petals, which crumbled and fell under her blouse.

Having loaded the wagon he silently climbed up and slowly turned towards home. The horses snorted, nodding their heads, and the wagon swayed easily from side to side. Suddenly it went a bit into a hole and lurched to the left.

"Pull on the bay! You can see it's a hole".

He cracked the whip over the horses. The horses jumped forward. That was his answer.

The wagon rolled unto a stone and tilted again.

"Pull on the black! How are you driving?"

Again he lifted his hand back as if to crack the whip, but at once lowered and tightly gripped the handle.

After a while:

"Watch out for the ditch! What's with you today? Are you trying on purpose to tip over the wagon, or is it that you just can't drive?"

The young man suddenly stopped the horses, jumped up, and, grabbing her, threw her from the wagon to the ground.

The sun then began to shine even more hotly; the young man began to sweat. And the crickets were chirping so terribly loudly all around.

She sat on the ground. She straightened her skirt around her legs, and then slowly got up. He still could not see her face.

He jumped from the wagon and ran to her.

"Did I hurt you badly?" In his voice was regret and shame and something else.

She was silent. She leaned up against his shoulder and looked somewhere far away. She was pensive and sad.

"No . . ." she said softly, forgivingly.

"Tell me, did I hurt you badly?"

"You're so . . ." She looked him in the eyes and began to smile. Then she again gazed at him for a long time with amazed eyes.

"Are you so very mad at me?"

"Where did you get that scar on your face?"

"Tell me, Anelė, did . . .?"

"You probably fight a lot?"

"Yes, that's from a knife . . ."

A pause.

"You're very cruel . . ." she said quietly, bemusedly, and caressed his shoulder, the rough shirt.

* * *

Sunday morning he washed so assiduously that the rough homemade soap almost ate out his eyes. He so painstakingly brushed his boots that the boot top reflected his face. "This time, even the clothes will have to be brushed," he was thinking. Then he washed his feet in the pond. With soap.

He crossed the yard mouthing a cigarette, his hat at an angle, and sat on the veranda.

"Well, what are you going to bring me from the town?" asked Anelė from the flower garden. "You always bring something for others, but never anything for me. And I try so hard to load wagons well for you."

The young man frowned at her. He kept chewing on his cigarette and remained silent. Here again came her smile. Ah, that half-open eye! Well, just wait . . .

"So you don't plan to bring me anything?" She came up to him and adorned his jacket lapel with a red flower, then coldly turned and walked into the drawing room.

He followed her with his eyes but did not even glance at the flower. He now remembered his wallet. He spat out the cigarette, slowly stood up and went inside.

The maid was busying herself around the stove; the farmer was washing up, splashing water. He had hung his jacket near the door.

The maid glanced at the young man and grinned. He frowned and looked at her, looked at the flower in his lapel, and quickly hid it in his pocket. Then he went along the wall, glanced at the farmer, looked at his jacket, stopped for a moment near where the jacket was hanging and quickly moved away.

Breakfast for some reason he couldn't eat at all. He took a few bites, put the spoon down and left.

He walked through the yard with unusual haste and somehow strangely hanging his head. Keeping his hand in his pocket. With the red rose.

* * *

Having returned home, he glanced at the drawing room window: nothing to be seen. Just flowers on the table. He went out into the orchard — empty. He was upset. Irritated. Suddenly on a bench under an apple tree he noticed a scarf. A vague happiness, but also an irritation, so that his heart had started to beat so violently. He stopped. He did not know, now, where to go further.

"Home already?" He became entirely confused upon hearing that voice and turned around. She was hiding from the sun in a lilac bush.

"So I came home . . ."

"You'll be hungry. We'll go, I'll get you something".

"No."

"Are you in a hurry to go somewhere?"

"Well, there is this dance. They invited . . ."

A pause.

"She doesn't even mention this morning's conversation' he thought to himself.

"What's new in town?"

"Nothing. A lot of people. The shops are full."

"What did you buy, if the shops are full of people?"

"Nothing. Well ..." A pause. "Please forgive me that I hurt you so . . ." He pulled a red necklace from his pocket.

"For which girl?"

"For you. You asked for a present, so I brought this back for you."

He held the necklace out to her.

She looked at him inquiringly; held out her hand, but did not even glance at the necklace. She held it with her lowered hand and was silent. Only after a long while did she remember and thank him. Again both were silent.

"Go and eat," she finally uttered sadly and went ahead of him. For some reason, she was deeply moved.

"Anelė, are you angry?"

"No, Jonas."

He caught up her hand and firmly pressed it. He looked at her deep eyes. Sad now, full of sympathy as well as of misty joy.

"What is it? Anelė, tell me . . ."

At this time Anelė's young neighbor, Andrius, her intended, entered the yard and stopped in amazement.

"Leave me in peace!" she suddenly retorted bitterly and went to the guest.

Andrius still remained silent and, frowning, glanced at Jonas and at the necklace in her hand. Anelė was momentarily at a loss, then smiled somewhat disdainfully and suddenly burst out laughing.

"Imagine: this young man won't leave me alone," she justified herself. "He thinks he can court me, as if I were a hired maid. That's just too much. Take a look at what he brought me today." Still laughing loudly, she showed him the red necklace.

Andrius was still standing wrathful and silent.

Jonas disappeared. He was beaten, ground into the dirt.

Suddenly he quickly strode from the granary across the yard. Passing them he halted and was completely pale. With a voice full of hate he screamed in Andrius' face:

"That's right, that's a present for last night, spent together in the granary."

He walked quickly off through the gate onto the road.

"Let's go, let's go . . ." she clutched Andrius' hand. "Let's go into the drawing room, I'll explain . . ."

She was trembling.

Leaving her guest in the drawing room, she ran into another room to "freshen up." She threw the necklace on the table and turned all red from anger. With this pin from her hair she would stab out his eyes. She would bite his hand to the blood.

She tore apart the necklace and let the beads fall to the floor.

But after having said good-bye to Andrius, she picked them up and strung them together, smiling sadly and almost in tears.

* * *

During lunch into the servants' room entered the farmer. He stood at the table and looked for a long time at the young farm hand.

102

"Well, Jonas, how much do I still owe you?"

Jonas slowly put down his spoon, looked somewhere to the side and stood up.

"You know how much," he answered, taking his cap from the hook.

"So, take this. It's minus the amount you took yourself."

Without saying a word Jonas put the money in his pocket and went to pack his things.

As he was crossing the yard, his hat pulled over his eyes, Anelė stopped him near the gate.

"Jonas . . ."

He stopped, glanced briefly at her and, looking at the ground, asked,

"Well, what?"

"You won't leave . . ."

Her father was standing on the veranda and stared at them balefully. He bit his lips but did not dare to say anything because the hired people were in the house and the windows were open. But Anelė suddenly ran to her father, grasped his arm and spoke quickly, breathlessly.

"He can't leave, father!"

"He can't leave?" her father said in amazement. He could barely control his anger.

"No, I won't marry Andrius. I can't . . ."

Her father looked at her and his eyelashes trembled.

"I can't . . . Because . . . because Jonas was with me in the granary . . ."

As if burned with hot iron, her father grabbed her by the arm and dragged her from the veranda into the drawing room, locking the door.

Jonas ran up to the door. Inside he heard heavy blows and soft moans. He beat upon the door to no avail. His knuckles were bruised and bloody, and he was soaked with sweat.

After a while the door opened. Her father came out and stopped in the doorway. Clenching his teeth he glared at the young man. He wanted to say something, his lips trembled, but he regained control of himself.

"Ah, the devil with you, but you can stay," he finally uttered, breathless. He strode quickly past Jonas, stopped, gave him a heavy blow across the face, and went into the yard.

Jonas stood motionless for a long moment and then cautiously stepped into the drawing room. Anelė was standing at the mirror fixing her disheveled hair. Her left hand was blue and on the floor lay a cane of reed.

"What's happening, Anelė?"

"I don't know myself."

A pause.

"I told him I would not marry Andrius. But you know that," she said coming towards him.

"You won't marry him?"

"How can I marry him? I don't want him. And you yourself said that you've been in the granary . . ." She looked him right in the eyes. Her white teeth were clenched, her lips open. Her eyes kept getting smaller and were strangely shining.

"But that was a lie, Anelė"

"Oh, yes, I also tricked father. Don't you understand?" Suddenly she put her arms around him and kissed him for a long time.

"Well, this was that kiss you wanted so badly," she said barely able to speak. And her lips were dry and hot.

And so, within two weeks or so, they were married.

* * *

Vincas Ramonas (b. 1905 Lithuania, d. 1985 Chicago) was a schoolteacher in Lithuania. During World War II, he fled the Soviet invasion and eventually settled in Chicago. This short story (original Lithuanian language title, 'Linu ziedai') was first published in 1934 in a collection of his short stories entitled *Dailininkas Rauba*. ("As a new type of artistic thought, based on impressionistic and expressionistic poetry, the short story collection *Dailininkas Rauba* saw its debut (1934), which describes the life of various social groups in Lithuania."[1]) This translation was published in *Lituanus*, the Lithuanian Quarterly Journal of Arts and Sciences Vol. 30 No. 1 (Spring 1984).

---

[1]   E-leidykla.lt, Vincas Ramonas (http://www.eleidykla.lt/ rasyk/rasytojai/vincas-ramonas.html) (accessed Feb. 13, 2009) (translated from the original Lithuanian by Tadas Klimas).

THE IDLER

Aloyzas Baronas

Translated by Tadas Klimas

When a series of foreign armies of occupation come to despoil a land and deport or enslave its people, one would think it would be silly and futile for people to continue to try to hold onto their property, or, more importantly, to make distinctions amongst their compatriots according to their relative wealth and social status.
This is, I think, a lesson which many Lithuanians learned during the events of the Second World War and thereafter.
But what if a person had already learned this lesson, had known it from the start?

They all called him an idler, though he, like other men, had a home and sometimes a job. He was comparatively still pretty young, and one might say, even handsome; someone had said he had even studied somewhat. Nevertheless, he was an idler. And he could not think of any way to elude that name, although he loved to think, to ponder. He would sit down near his broken down little house (that the village council had ten times condemned to be razed) and would watch people in the near-by marketplace haggle over a few pennies that seemed to him terribly unnecessary, and he would attempt to divine whether he was such a 'bum' simply because he did not need money. In no way could he understand why he necessarily had to dress well and have money in order not to be a bum. And he had also heard that some philosopher had written many books while sitting in a barrel.

The idler would look at his wooden shoes, at his socks that stuck out of those shoes, at his extremely shiny pants, at his short, coarse cloth jacket, and he would wonder whether clothes change the heart. For he wasn't naked, and to be poorly dressed is certainly no evil. Sometimes he would go lie down in a field;

he'd watch as an insect would climb up a long piece of grass, or a wagtail with its long legs would leap in search of something. The sun would beat up the idler's back, and he would roll over on his other side.

"So you say you're sunning yourself, eh, John?" one of his acquaintances would say.

"Yes, I am. And why shouldn't I sun myself if there is a lot of sun and a lot of time?"

"You're lazy if you have so much time. Work calls."

"I can work or not work: for I do no wrong to any soul by not working."

"But you could earn some money; you could get some clothes and begin looking like a person."

"'Like a person,' you say? It seems to me that I already look like a person. And I really don't think the birds would sing more sweetly, or the sun would shine more brightly, if I were to dress better. Moreover, it's good to live like this."

"But you're in rags and often hungry!"

"Therefore I am free. I need no watch, I have no job in which I must quarrel or nag, nor must I try to trick a friend in the market. Here one watches the flowers bloom, one listens to the birds singing, one suns oneself and wonders about something — for instance, why the sky is blue?"

"Ah, you're always singing the same old song," the acquaintance would say in parting, and would thank God that he's smart and clothed, and that he holds some sort of place in life. And he would be happy that he doesn't occupy the lowest position on this earth — for that position belonged to the idler.

"They all say the same thing," the idler would remark as he'd watch the other man leave. "They have a lot of money and many worries. They each want to live better than the other. They all think about the future, but not one of them thinks about the past. For isn't the past now the same for all of us? Whether you scattered money or ran about to gather it in, whether you were a laborer or a scientist, a king or a farmer: now it's all only the past, and today it's not any bit better for you that sometime ten years ago you wore an expensive suit, lived in a fine house — or in a dilapidated shack."

The idler would observe the sun and the fog, and he would listen to the churchbells toll, but he could not understand why they called him a bum simply because he tried to be free from money. "You bum!" kids would shout as they'd race past him on their way home from school. First laughter would come over him, and then anger, that even the young are taught to constrain their lives with meaningless trivia.

Later on, everything took a very bad turn for the worse. Foreign soldiers came, read speeches, hung flags up, photographed his shack (then knocked it down without building a new one) and told stories about great freedom and a fabulous life.

"Now you'll be able to be a big shot," some of his neighbors told him.

"And why should I be a big shot? The sun will not shine the more for that, nor will birds sing more prettily, nor will summer be warmer, nor will the years be better. For isn't it good to live without a clock, without being in service to anything, without money?"

Then other soldiers marched in and began destroying all that the first soldiers had overlooked.[1] Now it would sometimes be

---

[1] Trans. note: The 'first soldiers' are those of the Soviets; the first invasion and occupation of Lithuania was by Germany's then-ally, Soviet Russia. The

that the idler could not lie in the sun or wade through the white snow in his big wooden shoes just whenever he fancied.

But one time someone said to him, "It's all very easy for you, John, you being a derelict bum. You have nothing and so have nothing to lose."

"I have more than all of you put together, for I am free from wealth," he would answer while happily remarking under his breath, "Well, at least this once they're jealous of me. They should have become jealous of me long ago, for I understand life in a different way then they do. I can give up everything that burdens the shoulders and the heart; that tears at the pockets. I once had a house. Now I don't even have that. But of that I'm glad, for while I had one house, now I have the whole world. And so I live, without a wish to be something great. Never will I be the first — and never will I fall, for I never climb up high. I'll never scramble for a place or for some money — but I'll never escape the name of tramp, or idler, of bum."

As the idler had foreseen, someone called him those names again. They called him those names at a time when it should have been clear to everyone that we would all soon become bums, idlers, vagrants.

"Even an idler has a heart, and many that aren't idlers have money where there hearts should be," the idler replied angrily, but at once becoming sorry for his words. "Please forgive me for getting mad. After all, the entire world can't live as I do. Maybe I really am a bum."

Then the first soldiers started to push the second soldiers out. These resisted and forced everyone to resist. Late one morning the idler, lying amid a clump of raspberry bushes, saw gray-faced and gray-uniformed soldiers herding one of the idler's

---

second soldiers are those of the Germans, who also invaded Lithuania. To the Lithuanians, both were foreign, invading armies.

neighbors into a truck containing many men of various ages and attires, all of whom were silent as death. The neighbor's wife caught hold of a soldier's hand and that of her husband.

"No, I need workers. Give me another in your place, and I'll let your husband go," spoke the soldier in an unclear tongue.

But the idler understood, and, emerging from the bushes, said, "I'll go in his stead."

"The bum!" cried the neighbor's wife. "Oh — it's you, John!" She corrected herself hurriedly. "I'll be grateful for the rest of my life."

"You can take a bag of clothes and food," observed the soldier.

"I don't have anything," answered the idler, stepping up into the truck with his heavy wooden shoes.

"We should at least give him some shoes," said the neighbor while quickly putting distance between himself and the truck.

"Well — we might still need them ourselves; we don't know how we'll have to live; maybe we'll still have to flee," the wife replied, recovering as if back from the grave.

And it's good that they didn't burden the idler with this and that, for he — more than ever — had no need of anything. As they drove to work, airplanes attacked the column of motor vehicles and destroyed the trucks and the people.

Later someone related that he had seen the idler lying on his back along a ditch by the side of a road, in the sun, with his arms flung out wide as if wanting to say,

"How good it is to live and die when one's hands are empty."

* * *

111

Aloyzas Baronas (b. 1917 Lithuania, d. 1980 Chicago). Baronas attended university in Lithuania and later, having fled the Soviet occupation, in Germany. From 1955 he was an editor of the Lithuanian daily newspaper *Draugas*, published in Chicago. This translation was published in *Lituanus*, the Lithuanian Quarterly Journal of Arts and Sciences (Vol. 27, No. 4 Winter 1981).

DID THE DEVIL?

Jurgis Jankus

Translated by Tadas Klimas

Lithuania's fate in the last several hundred years has been a hard one. The events of World War II, with the successive occupations by foreign powers leading to a fifty year occupation by the Soviet Union, complete with mass deportations and a nearly ten year guerilla war, was an especial ordeal.
One can wonder, Why? What did Lithuania do to deserve this? Probably nothing is the answer.
But what if someone, some being who ought really to know, offered to tell you the reason?

All of them can think what they want, can say what they want. I could care less. That's everyone's personal opinion, and each to his own. But no one will convince me it never happened. Though even when they say, okay, it really happened, they explain it as having been a dream, a delirium, your basic fantasy, the result of self-deception or even of self-hypnosis, like one young psychologist tried very hard to convince me. She said that, especially at my age, all sorts of subconscious self-hypnosis can occur.

Well, I suppose it might have been some sort of a dream. Dreams can be completely outlandish, and I might have had one of those. But one muddle just refuses to leave me alone: you see, even the sharpest dreams fade away for me with time. The memory remains that it occurred, that I did have such a dream, but all of the acuteness, all the details, fade away; they entwine themselves into a fog of things forgotten until from the whole experience, which might have been extremely life-like, there remains just the simple thought that sometime something was dreamed. Finally, even this remembrance grows dull.

But nothing changes with this particular memory. Every detail, even every word is still as alive and clear as it was then.

I don't know anything about self-delusion or self-hypnosis, so I don't want to argue with experts in those disciplines. I don't want to afford them some sweet fun at the expense of my ignorance, but even they can't convince me that I could hypnotize myself as a result of just slipping into a reverie. Especially not me, whom a professional once tried and failed to hypnotize. She tried, too, that young psychologist I just mentioned. But she wasn't able to, either. She blamed her failure on my age-diminished capacity. Maybe some little devil tempted me into saying, "Guess I'm suffering from calcified perception." She thought about this for a moment and then smiled. "You know, that's not a bad name for it. Not bad at all," she added, and that's how we parted. She with my new term, which she may never use, and me with my doubts.

You know, sometimes I even try to make myself believe that it's possible to think so deeply about something, that one's thoughts become reality. Real, seeable, hearable, touchable. But I can't. I don't know about you, but me, I think up all sorts of nonsense. Some of it is even embarrassing to admit to myself. Especially at night if I can't get to sleep. Often this insomnia is in fact caused by these little things that one starts to think about. Some nothing gets into your head, something else joins it, then something else again. Entire histories begin to form, about which you'd never breathe a word to someone else; but with these, like some enchantment, you speed through the night. Of course, one always puts oneself at the center of these stories, and everything else revolves around you, like the spokes of a wheel around its hub. You wind up who-knows-where with that whole gang, but you always know what's happening, you always understand, perhaps with some regret, that it all is a hurtling, uncontrollable effect of your mind that has nothing in common with reality or with the flow of daily events. These ravings are strong enough to chase sleep away, but are far and away from any hypnosis, and they never become a reality which one could touch with a finger. But this time it was different. It was just as real as my sitting here, trying to commit this conundrum to paper. But, so that everything would fall into place, let me start from further back.

My childhood friend Chirbulis — everybody used to call him Chirby back then for some reason — was going to celebrate his eightieth birthday in Chicago and had invited me to fly over and celebrate it with him. He said in a few years he won't bow out from doing the same for me. He added that I should book a flight only one way, because after a week one of his friends would be driving to New York City, so he could take me and drop me off in Rochester. And if it wouldn't be too inconvenient, he would like to fly over and spend a day or two. It would be a good occasion for him to see a new city, and it'll save a good chunk of cash. He wrote me so himself, and while we were toasting his eightieth, his friend said the same. His friend, a cheerful dzukas[1] who never seemed to sit still and was always shooting his camera off in all directions, really wanted to see the city of Kodak and especially Kodak itself, on whose products he'd spent more than a few thousand dollars. But then everything changed. My suitcases were stuffed so full of Lithuanian sausages and books you can't get in Rochester that I could hardly lift them, when he, all of a sudden, ran off to Wisconsin to go fishing with who knows who and without telling me a thing. He only let me know through some third parties that hell wouldn't break loose if I were to wait in Chicago for another week or so until he'd return with some salmon, or maybe even some sturgeon. Rochester, he said, will still be there, but a man can't get up into Wisconsin just any time he likes. One has to luck out and find someone who knows where, when, and how.

---

[1] Translator's note: "dzukas" denotes a person from the southern part of Lithuania.

Chirbulis halfheartedly tried to talk me into staying, but I just didn't want to use up any more of my friend's hospitality. I could have gone home by plane, but suddenly, for some reason, I got a hankering to try the train. I had plenty of time, and I couldn't even remember the last time I had ridden a train. I had the whole day before the train, so, poking around in my friend's giant book collection, I came across a book that he'd probably brought over from Germany: Thomas Mann's *Joseph und seine Brueder*. I came across it and was hooked. I had read many of Mann's books, but I had only vaguely heard of Joseph and his brothers. It would always somehow slide through my fingers. This time I got hold of it and turned page after page, although I knew I'd never even get it half done by the time I had to go, let alone finish it. Finally, I screwed up the courage to ask him if I could borrow it for the trip home, saying I'd send it back to him. You see, I knew very well he never lent any books to anyone, not even his closest friends. He would just say, "I'm not a lending library." But this time, without even saying a word, he took the book, opened it up to the title page, and wrote:

"In memory of our days of youth and happiness." He thought for a moment and added: "And of what may be the last time we see each other on this earth."

When I tried to explain I felt bad, breaking apart the collection he had so carefully put together, he just waved his hand and gave me a sad smile. "A waste," he said. "Just a plain, old, selfish waste. You know, for the money I spent in loading my shelves, I could maybe have done some good for someone. But now ... You think they'll ever be useful to anyone? One fine day I'll be carried out feet first, and they'll wind up in the garbage. It appears it's hard for a man to change. I started to collect them over there, when there was a reason, when the country had been pining for world culture.

And I continued to collect them over here, because I had started over there and couldn't stop. It never even entered my mind that no one here would have any use for them. Over there, I think they could still be useful. People over there are still longing to know world culture. Maybe even more so now, than then, when they had the liberty to obtain these books. They'd carry them all out and away like something holy. Some would even learn other languages, just so they could read what they had brought home from that old man who'd just croaked. Just like we used to do, a long time ago. How many languages did we learn, just so we could read the originals, and here... Believe it or not, sometimes I stand here and look at my bookshelves and say, "Lord, how have our people offended You, that You should punish them so? And if this is not according to Your will, then can it be the Manicheans were right, and You are not the most powerful, but that beside you the Evil one is just as powerful as you, and that the two of you vie with one another, as equal against equal?"

Having said that, he pushed the book into my 'hands, adding that he wouldn't read so boring a thing a second time anyway, and that I'd be able to savor Mann's long sentences not only during the trip, but that it should last me for a while even after I'd get home.

I took it. Not only did I take it, but I gave him my truly heartfelt thanks. Long sentences had never bothered me, but would always put me in a peaceful mood, like a wide river's flow. I even feel that deeper thoughts fit more easily into long sentences than into nervous bits of chopped up speech. Once, jokingly, I had called a friend's overly short sentenced writing "short stuff," and, of course, with those two words I had put quite a bit of a chill into what had been a pretty warm friendship. What am I saying, a bit of a chill. There was nothing left of that friendship other than a hunk of ice.

While accepting the book, one of my strange habits didn't even come to mind: while traveling, I like to look around, I want to see everything. So, between the passing scenery and the lurching of the train, I wasn't able to spare Joseph much attention. Having gone some little distance, I even decided I would have been better off if I had brought along some short, light, adventure novel instead, and I sadly closed the covers on that calm story, woven throughout with deep thoughts, which I had been absolutely unable to integrate into the rumbling of the train and the flashing by of the scenery. Having put the book away, I gave myself up to the fading, sunset colors of the fields, to groups of black-checkered cows, to roads which came from far off and then, cutting across the railroad, would continue on to who-knows-where. And all of them empty, as if all the inhabitants had gone off at the same time to have dinner. For a while, a large thoroughfare paralleled the train track, and there was some traffic on it. I began to count the number of cars the train out sped. But one little green car just did not want to give in to the train. And it didn't give in. It sped along so evenly with the train alongside my window as if it had become part of it. And the driver wasn't a man, but a fair haired girl. I began to like her risky game, but also I started to worry that she would not stumble upon some policeman lurking for plunder. Judging from the way the train was passing the other cars, its speed had to have been at least eighty miles an hour, and she was supposedly limited to only fifty-five. I was completely on her side, and I wanted to wave to her through the window, but she always had her eyes riveted to the road. Eventually, some woods came to separate the train from the road, and I was left alone with the green of the forest and the rumbling of the train, and wondered whether the thoroughfare would come back to parallel the train, and whether there would still be upon it that woman, who was so determined not to lose her race.

No longer attracted by the sameness of the twilight, I reopened Joseph and all his brothers and the not-too-smart Egyptians.

"Is this seat taken?" a voice interrupted my attempt at reading.

I raised my eyes. Next to the empty seat stood a man, who looked like he had come right out of Isaac Bashevis Singer's *Satan in Goray* or Leib Peretz's *My Memoirs*: he was tall and lean, with a dark goatee and eyelids which seemed to have a rosy blush. His eyes, dark brown and very serious, nevertheless scintillated with puckishness. The train compartment was quite unsteady at that moment, so he was holding onto the seat back with his left hand. His right hand's fingers were tucked inside his coat between the two top buttons.

I am rather shy and I don't know how to make the acquaintance of people I come across while traveling. I think that's why I feel very uncomfortable when I have to sit shoulder to shoulder with someone for hours and not say a word. Being by oneself is more comfortable anyhow: You can lean any way you want, and even lie down across two seats. I cast my glance about the compartment. There were only a few people in it, and there were plenty of spare seats. I was about to say that the seat was taken, but that strange glint in his eye made me think he had chosen me for some prank, maybe even a mean one. He obviously knew the seat was free, and when I would say, it's taken, he'd have the pleasure of embarrassing me in some way. Maybe he'd label me an anti-Semite, or who-knows-what.

So I said it was free, and returned to my book. I read the same sentence several times, but I couldn't make heads or tails of it. I kept wondering what experiment he had chosen me for and why he had chosen me, when there were other people in the compartment.

With his appearance a smell — perhaps not a smell, but an oppressive miasma — seemed to settle over the compartment. Perhaps not the entire compartment, but only over our seats — but it was so real it seemed to push me straight down into Singer Goray's sauna. The sentence I was trying to read kept getting mixed up in my mind with a vision of Itse and his wild blond hair, who, before his wedding, was diving into the water seventy-two times. His diving was so rhythmic that it started to pull me in. I shut the book, I think I even shuddered, and turned towards the window. The woods had been left behind, but I couldn't see the road, only dark fields broken by black silhouettes of bushes and trees. Here and there a light would pierce the darkness, or automobile headlights would shine for a moment and then suddenly be gone. The headlights gave me a strange fancy, and I imagined that somewhere over there the blonde woman is still speeding along and is getting closer to a railroad station that is coming up soon. When we pull into the station, she'll run into my compartment and demand a seat, the one next to me of that traveler who seemed to be the author of that strange oppressive feeling.

"It must be pretty difficult to read such a hard book when the train is so unsteady. Maybe even impossible," my neighbor said, interrupting the ending of my reverie. I turned my head toward him.

"I really regret not having learned German while I was young. I read the English translation, but a translation is never the same as the original," he continued in the same voice, as if we had been old acquaintances. "I myself used to write a bit in Yiddish, and I'd be pretty pleased when I'd be translated into other languages. But some of them were translated into languages I could read, and when I'd read them, I often could hardly recognize my own stories. The nuances of my thoughts would disappear, many of the allusions would be different, and sometimes the thoughts I had had in mind when I had written the words in my native language would have been altered. In general, it was like a food that had lost its aroma."

I felt that my neighbor was not just an ordinary man, but perhaps somebody well-known, if his books had been translated into other languages. But my initial urge to caution had not yet passed. "The contents are the same, however," was my rather short answer.

He seemed to feel my caution, for he said, "I would like to ask you to forgive my wish to sit in this seat. If I had been in your place, I might even have said, why are you trying to squeeze in here when the car is half-empty. But you see when I saw old Joseph in your hands, well, I couldn't restrain myself. Nowadays very few people are interested in such books. As for its contents," he went on, not even waiting for any reply from me as to his apology, "Contents are facts. A mere recital of fact is not art. Even the lowest reporter can do that."

"But there can be art even in a news report," I interjected.

"Yes," he smiled, "but then it will not be truthful. Some truth will remain, of course, but it will be warped, made to be individual, no longer true."

"But what then is the true truth?" I asked, not letting up.

"The true truth?" he said, wrinkling his brow. Lights again flashed in his dark eyes. At that moment I stopped being sorry I had not relied originally that the seat next to me was taken. He continued:

"The truth, speaking in plain language, is that, which is, and it is in that way, in which it is, and not in that way in which all of us see it. The truth is the essence of a fact and its condition, and it is not our theories derived from the manifestations of that fact."

"So it would seem we are unable to see truth itself?" I interrupted. "But why? Are our eyes imperfect? Is our thought process defective? Or perhaps there really is no truth at all. Perhaps truth really is a mirage created by our ability to think and see that which we think about. In that case wouldn't truth be only something we fool ourselves with?"

My half-purposely thrown out series of questions clearly affected him: a shudder passed through him and even his whiskers rose up as if they were hung on an invisible string.

"You almost hit the bull's eye. Almost," he almost shouted and even made as if to jab me in the chest with his finger, but stopping halfway. He then continued to lecture in a completely calm voice: "It is probably not news to you, especially if you are a believer, that God made man in His own image. Not identical, but similar. No one has said just how similar. Perhaps only to the extent that He gave man the ability to create, to make something which had never existed before, but man — perhaps this will be a novel thought for you — man in his creative effort made a God who is exactly identical to man himself. Since there are no two human beings who are exactly alike, therefore everyone's God is always somewhat unique. Everyone's God is thus closer to the individual, but does that mean that there is no God?"

"Of course not," I quickly replied.

"You see," he gave a rather happy smile and stroked his hand over his thick beard. "If God's existence does not depend upon the many conceptions man has of him, that is to say, does not depend upon man's ability to see, to think, even upon the quickness of man's eye, then why should that determine the existence of truth, peace, love, and of many other eternal things?"

Here I had to do some thinking. I couldn't throw an intelligent reply together at once, but then he went on:

"Let us take that same Joseph for example. Everyone who wrote about him made him a bit different.

And Thomas Mann made him different from the other versions. Mann's translators also lent their own flavor to the matter. I would really like to know all of the languages into which Mann has been translated, then to get all of the translations and to read them all together. Line by line, page by page, chapter by chapter, and in this way to find out just how many different Josephs have been created and recreated in that same novel by man's creative capacity. Wouldn't that be an interesting experiment?"

But then my momentary block went away. "Yes, it would be interesting," I said, "But not for me. I have never been the type to splinter my toothpick so as to fill up an entire wagon with slivers. Having read the original, I doubt I would have the patience to read the translations. Even while reading the original, I am searching for something completely different. While reading the Bible, it came to me that Joseph was probably the first to institute slavery on a nationwide scale. And he did it in a very underhanded way. He did not create it through force or by some decree, like today's dictators would, but he forced the people themselves to become slaves so as not to starve to death. And isn't he the first person to have induced one entire nation to hate another? I wanted to see if Thomas Mann would confirm or disprove this idea, or would perhaps explain it in some other way, or perhaps, not having noticed anything, would touch upon it only glancingly."

These words of mine caused him to smile from ear to ear and he even slapped his knee.

"Come on, did you really think of that yourself? No one whispered anything to you?"

"No one," I answered, and feeling he had wanted to put me down on purpose with his question, I somewhat indignantly added, "Unless it were the evil spirit, so that I would understand where the roots of anti-Semitism lie."

Right after I said this, I became anxious, thinking that now he would really start in on me. But he didn't even blink and just kept right on going as if he hadn't heard me.

"The thing is, many never comprehend this. They read it and leave it alone. Everyone is happy that he saved not only Egypt but also his entire people. Even Joseph himself doesn't get it. By

123

the way, do you know what happened the other morning, when Israel's politicians threw Begin out of office? But no, you wouldn't know ... At that time the Lord God was walking with Joseph in the gardens of heaven. Joseph kept looking and looking at what was going on in Israel's parliament. He couldn't control himself any longer and turned to the Lord and cried, "Why do you allow your people to humiliate a man who has done so much good for them! Through his entire life nothing mattered to him but a free, independent Israel. How much did he toil and suffer for this, only to get this kind of reward from his countrymen?" The Lord smiled, "So what would you have me do?" he asked, shrugging his shoulders. Joseph shouted, "Stop these ignominious attacks upon a holy man of the people. Stop up the mouths of the demagogues, hypocrites, egomaniacs, and fools. Turn the liars' tongues to stone, open the eyes of the blind, so they would see the truth!" "Whose truth?" the Lord again smiled. Hearing this from the lips of the Almighty, Joseph became so amazed that his eyes turned into complete moons. "Whose? What do you mean, whose? Can it be this too must be explained to the Lord? Israel's truth. The eternal truth of Your chosen people," he answered all in one breath. "But the majority of Israel's parliament would be very unhappy," the Lord smiled again.

Joseph became even more incensed and now, completely enraged, shouted, "And what is it to You, Lord, if the unjust become unhappy? Let them take a lesson from this!" In answer to Joseph's explosion of anger. God answered very calmly, "And you, would it have been very pleasing to you if I had constrained you in the same manner?" Joseph was so shocked he drew back several steps on his heels and cried, "Lord, when? Why? When did I act not in accordance with your will?" "Why, when else but when you were saving Egypt from famine," God serenely reminded Joseph of the distant past, which in eternity is always very near. Joseph grew even more amazed. "But was this not your will, o Lord? Should I have disobeyed you and let the famine take the lives of the whole nation? And with them your chosen people?" "No, Joseph, no. Indeed, my will was for you to save them, but you substituted your will for mine. You gathered up, as I had instructed you, the fifth part gratis, but then you distributed it not as charity but for payment, until you had taken everything from the starving. And when they no longer had any possessions with which to buy their bread, you took their very selves. You enslaved free people to the state. You only raised up your own relatives. It was not enough for you to have saved them from famine, but you forced the enslaved true owners of the nation to serve them. In this manner you made the entire Egyptian nation hate your clan."

"And you know what happened then. I myself had to intercede that your clan would not be annihilated by the hatred you yourself had created. I had to send Moses. You see, Joseph, the relations of men are to me like the waves of an ocean. They arise, cast themselves upon the shore, then recede, sweeping much off with them and disappearing in the ocean's expanse. Sometimes I regret having given man not only the power to create, but also the will to create according to their fancy. But I never regret not having given them absolute power, for they would have wiped each other out long ago. Perhaps including me as well. Is it any clearer now?" He added, but Joseph would not have been a true son of his people if he had left it at that.

Joseph frowned and said, "As far as I am concerned, o Lord, all right. It was long ago, and I loved all my relatives very much. Even my brothers, who had sold me. Perhaps from this love I thought You Yourself want the same thing as do I. Through my love I did not understand Your true will. Nevertheless You did not punish me, you allowed me to die in honor and contentment. But what has Begin done that he must suffer abasement and rejection? Is it just that he loved his people, that he wanted them to be free?"

Shadows of sadness appeared on God's bright face. "So, Joseph, we have arrived at the heart of the matter. If you haven't learned from your experience even over so many ages, then what can one expect of poor Begin and from many others, a list of whom would stretch from the beginning of time to its end. They all love and continue to love themselves, but not man, their own people, but not people. Just their own. Just themselves. Only their own people, only their own truth. If I would not know this, I would not dare to claim that some wave would not come and sweep Israel away into the sea of mankind, like it came after the crucifixion of my son." With these words God turned away and went off into the vastnesses of heaven.

Joseph remained standing there as if nailed to the spot. He thought and thought, and still he couldn't understand how it could be bad to help one's kinsmen. And if it is evil, then why didn't God tell him so at once, but instead waited for who knows what? If Joseph were too simple to understand this, then what hope do we have?"

My neighbor finished telling his long story, lowered his head, rested his chin on his chest, and appeared to be deep in thought. He probably was thinking about his own truth, which perhaps is not everywhere identical to my own, just like it differs from that of the Lord God. He leaned back from his ruminations, lifting his head up, took his hat off, looked at its gray silk lining, and swiftly put it back on his head. I wondered whether while lost in thought he had forgotten that his religion forbids him to be indoors without his head covered. I don't know where the courage came from to ask him, "Do you know where Lithuania is?"

"I know," he said without batting an eye and added, "Probably not less well then you do."

That not-less-well just about took my courage away. I thought perhaps he was from Vilnius, perhaps some professor from Telsiai, with whom I might fall into some meaningless argument as to who shot whom and who didn't shoot whom, who betrayed whom and who didn't betray whom, but having started I determined to keep going.

"And do you know that a red wave has washed over Lithuania? Has washed over her and is striving to wash the entire nation out into the wastes of Russia? Wash her there and sink her."

"I know that very well.",

"From your story of Joseph's conversation with God I understand, that Jews suffered and are suffering from an exaggerated concern for themselves. Let me tell you that when you asked me if that seat was taken I wanted to say it was taken, because who wants to sit squeezed together with a stranger when half the compartment is empty, but I was afraid to. I was afraid to open my mouth, so that you would not accuse me of being that which I am not. That you would not raise your voice and tell the whole compartment that here is yet another anti-semite, probably some Nazi accomplice. And who wants that. Perhaps you yourselves don't know you have really frightened people with that anti-semitism, that some are afraid to open their mouths even when they really should. At this moment a rather funny thought has come to my mind, but taking courage I'll tell it to you: if Israel's parliament knew what God said to Joseph the other morning, they would even call God an anti-semite. But forgive me. I have gotten away from what I had wanted to say. When I started, this is what I wanted to ask you: As far as I can see, Lithuania has never done anyone any sizeable hurt or evil. Indeed, through the ages Lithuania has herself suffered much. So what is the reason for her having to undergo such suffering? After all, even towards the Jews through the ages Lithuania has done only good, although they are trying hard to make her the scapegoat for the sins of others. If you heard what God said to Joseph, then perhaps you might have heard what God said, for example, to Vytautas, Mindaugas, perhaps even St. Casimir?"

My fellow traveler suddenly smiled as if he knew a great deal which I couldn't even begin to guess. He didn't even become angry at all the worn-out comments I'd made. He just rubbed his hands together in delight, and his eyes lit up as if to say, "Well, buddy, now you're going to hear something beyond your wildest dreams."

"You see, my friend, that's a whole different story," he began, taking hold of his beard with his right hand. "Completely different. The engines of every particular nation's life and death are somewhat dissimilar, but that of your nation is altogether unique. Many nations and even individuals suffer for what they have done, but very few for what they should have done, but did not do. Your nation is one of those few which did not do something which would have put them on a completely different path. This is hidden in the secrets of history and pre-history, but if God allows, I will tell you," taking hold of my shoulder with his hand he began whispering in my ear as if afraid someone might overhear this great secret, "But only you. No one else. And if you tell anyone else, don't tell them who told you. No one would believe you. Tell them you thought of it yourself. And now brace yourself," he said and gripped my shoulder even more tightly. He even gave me a little shake.

"Get ready. Rochester."

I lifted my eyes up to see the conductor leaning over and waking me up. Where my mysterious fellow traveler had been sitting was just an empty seat.

"Where did my friend get off? Buffalo?" I asked.

"Rochester," he repeated, and I understood he didn't know what I was talking about.

He couldn't understand, because I had spoken to him in Lithuanian. The same language in which I had just been speaking with the stranger. That's when I remembered that we hadn't even introduced ourselves. Neither had told the other who we were, and now he had disappeared without even leaving me his name.

When I asked the conductor again, this time in English, he became somewhat astonished and said, "I walked by here several times and I didn't see anyone sitting there. You were sleeping all the way from Toledo."

I tried to explain. "There was a rather dark haired man here, with a beard, sideburns, and a hard black hat."

The conductor made a face and shook his head. "I haven't seen anybody like that on the whole train."

Turning away, he added, "Here's Rochester."

I felt the train begin to slow. I grabbed my coat and suitcase, and noticed Joseph which had fallen to the floor. I picked it up, put it in my pocket, and carefully looked around the compartment. It was half-empty and my eye found no one even remotely similar to him who had sat next to me. The conductor can say what he wants, but I know what I know. For a moment considered I might have been dreaming, but I put this thought aside at once, because there aren't any dreams like this. There can't be. Everything was too clear, A dream wouldn't have occurred in that same compartment, even in that same seat. But where did he disappear to? Who was he? What's the truth?

I exited the compartment looking over my shoulder. I even checked the bathroom while walking by. I said to myself, maybe he went off with someone to have a cigarette, or, just to play games with me, was hiding somewhere. But the bathroom was empty and he wasn't in the smoking car. There wasn't anyone resembling him on the nearby empty platform, either. But a strange feeling had come over me and wouldn't let me go. A feeling that he was somewhere close with his Cheshire grin and that he was staring me right in the eyes with his own eyes, brown eyes behind reddened eyelids, eyes strangely sparkling as if to say I have never, ever, seen, not even in my wildest dreams, anything like what those eyes have seen and what they know.

The train car had stopped pretty far from the door of the station and my suitcase, crammed with books and Chicago-style sausages, was pulling my arm down more with every step, so, seeing an open path, I turned and went directly over to the parking lot, hoping to find a taxi still waiting there. I turned and stopped short. I even put my suitcase down and wiped my hand across my face. For a fleeting moment I wasn't sure whether I wasn't still sitting somewhere on a train and dreaming one of those strange dreams during which one wakes up and falls back asleep several times, because from over in back of the train station I saw an automobile pull out and drive away — the same light green car with the same blonde driving it whom I had seen through the window racing with the train.

Suddenly the green car stopped and its blonde driver turned her head towards me. She looked at me a moment, then waved and jumped out of her car. She hurried over to me, and I, not knowing what to do, probably just stood there open mouthed.

"So hello there," said a happy and familiar voice, and I could feel the veil dropping from my eyes.

My friend's young wife Broné was standing in front of me.

"Why didn't you let us know when you were coming back? We would have waited for you. As it was, we didn't really know when. Good thing I saw you standing there, or I would have blown out of here by myself. I just dropped Vytautas off. He's on his way to Boston for one of those organizations of his, a conference or something. Here, let me grab your suitcase."

"No, no, I'll handle it."

But she grabbed it first, lifted it off the pavement and dropped it back down.

"What's this?" she laughed in surprise. "Did you bring some bricks with you? Well, don't kill yourself. I'll bring the car closer."

She ran off, brought the car over, we lifted the suitcase in, and moved out from the station.

She was talking of what was new in Rochester and asked me what I had seen in Chicago, and I kept feeling that the perhaps-dreamed, perhaps-real stranger was sitting quietly there in the back seat, waiting for a chance to tell me the reason Lithuania is suffering. What she had not done and so earned her punishment. Not able to control myself I looked over my shoulder several times although I knew I wouldn't see anyone there. Wanting to dispel this unnerving feeling, I decided to tell her what I had seen on the train.

"If I didn't see you here in front of me, I'd swear I'd seen you racing with the train," I said, and she shot me a look of astonishment.

"Really?" she asked.

"Absolutely. A car just like this and a woman who looked exactly like you were racing the train. I can even say now that your hair styles are identical, except that maybe hers was a little more tousled by the wind."

"It probably really was me," she laughed. "I was also racing."

"But not all the way near Chicago," I objected in surprise.

"I don't know. Maybe I was somewhere close to there. After I packed Vytautas' things for him, I sat down on the sofa. Suddenly I got so sleepy, it was even sweet. I drew a pillow down under my head and, I guess I fell asleep and even dreamed. I'm driving down a road and a train is rushing by next to me. It wants to pass me, but I say, no, no way. It speeds up, I speed up, it speeds up, I speed up. Then the road ran into some woods and it ended. All I saw in front of me were trees. I let go of the wheel, covered my face with my hands, screamed and woke up. I guess I really screamed pretty loud, because Vytautas even rushed in from the yard. He thought somebody had gotten in and was trying to kill me. He was afraid to leave me to go to Boston. He finally did leave, but ordered me to lock everything up tight and be careful.

That dream of hers mixed me up even worse. Where did this coincidence come from? While I was traveling she never came to mind. I don't even remember thinking about her while I was in Chicago. Unless my whole trip on the train was nothing but a dream, or "self-hypnosis," that catch-phrase that can explain anything. If this wasn't a glimpse by a mortal, standing on the edge of eternity, of those vast spaces in which there will be no mysteries, then I'll agree to put this episode down to simple calcification of the old frontal lobes, or perhaps just to the beginning of their calcification.

But if so, then who of us can ever tell what is and is not the truth?

* * *

Jurgis Jankus was born in Lithuania in 1906. He already enjoyed an excellent reputation as a novelist in pre-war Lithuania when he had to flee his homeland to escape the Soviet occupation. Settling in Rochester, New York, he worked in factories and raised four boys with his wife, Kotryna. He wrote at night and on the weekends, and published a number of collections of short stories and two plays. In 1991 he traveled to Lithuania, which had newly re-established its independence, for the first time since WWII. There he greatly enjoyed the many literary events which were organized in his honor. Jurgis Jankus died in 2002 and is buried in Rochester, New York.

This short story appeared in a collection of Jankus' short stories, *Tėvas Venancijus ir jo Matilda* (Lietuviškos knygos klubas 1988). Its title in the original was *Sukalkėjusi percepcija, ar?* Its translation into English was published under the title, *Calcified Perception, Or?* in *Lituanus*, the Lithuanian Quarterly Journal of Arts and Sciences, Vol. 41, No. 2 (Summer 1995).

BARBORYTĖ

Jurgis Jankus

Translated by Tadas Klimas

All men die. As do all women, including very old women. But few very old women are also bestest, bestest, inseparable buddies with young children, in this case, a young boy. Even fewer laugh on their deathbed, a laugh of innocence which might, just might, even save some souls.

That morning Barborytė had taken her seat at the breakfast table along with the rest of us, but she had eaten very little. After having sat for a while, she had eaten perhaps half a spoonful of beat soup. Then she had looked out the window at the cherry tree, which had just sprouted swollen pink buds, and had said quietly, as if to herself,

'Well, how time flies! It seems just yesterday that the leaves were falling, and now Daratelė's cherry tree is thinking about blossoms. And the woodpecker — Mikey! Look, look! Do you see how he is fixing his nest? And you, Verutė, make sure today is only a half-day for the child. The woodpecker brought it on his tail, already, and he brought the wagtail as well.[1] Look at the wagtail strutting up and down on the fence. The woodpecker brought both on its tail — the wagtail and the half-day.'

We all got up from the table and went to look through the windows. And truly, in Tverkaus' oak the woodpecker was getting its nest ready. Right then, there was only one of them, but we knew that soon another would appear. It was like that every spring. We stared without glancing away, and the

---

[1] Trans. note: A wagtail is a small Old World bird which constantly moves its tail.

woodpecker perhaps wanting to say hi! to its home, or perhaps simply from joy that it had found its nest safe and sound, threw its head back and, having wiggled its neck, began to peck at the tree. It pecked at it so long and with so much energy that the joy of the spring which had arrived took my breath away. A bit of a wild energy grabbed at me as well, and I wanted to strut and run around, like the woodpecker, and only the only thing holding me back from strutting around was knowing that the rest of them would laugh and say I'm nuts.

'Oh Jesus!' my mother shouted, making us all jump, and as if on a hot plate we all jumped back from the windows.

We were all focused on the woodpecker and so we hadn't seen when Barborytė had moved away from the window. Now we say she was at the end of the table, holding on to one of its legs, all hunched over. If it weren't for the table leg, she would have been out flat on the floor. My father bent over, picked her up like a child and carried her to bed.

'Run as fast as you can, go get Mortutė,' my mother urged me.[2]

I still stood around a bit, wanting to see if Barborytė is really dying, but my mother pushed me towards the door, adding,

'Just run, and no goofing around, so that God would not call her without a decent send-off.'

I ran off as fast as I could. I really didn't want Barborytė to go away without a good send-off, as if she were some sort of non-believer.

---

[2] Trans. note: Lithuanian has two forms similar to the English familiar form, e.g., *Johnny*. Mortutė's given name is *Morta*, and the familiar form used here renders it *Mortutė*, which could be loosely translated as 'little Morta.' Similarly, Barborytė's given name would be *Barbora*, and *Barborytė* is the familiar.

Mortutė was an old woman. Of course, back then all older women seemed to me to be very old. She had never married, and was called by some a spinster, by others a *davatka*—that is, an overly 'devout' woman. But in our home she was simply 'Mortutė.' She lived alone in a poorly-built hut, she knew all of the prayers by heart, ones for every sort of calamity or unfortunate circumstance, such as after a fire, or at the side of a person who had drowned, for every sort of illness, and for those who were dying. The most important were those for the dying, because these traveled at once to the ear of the Lord God, and when the soul of the deceased reached Him, the Lord already knew what had happened in our vail of tears. Even Saint Peter knew beforehand, when to open up the gates of heaven, so that the soul of the deceased person would not have to wait in the cold.

All of this had been told to me by Mortutė a couple of times, because this was not the first time for Barborytė. She had been unconscious already several times, and several times she had been given the send-off, but after Mortutė's prayers she had gotten better as if touched by a miraculous hand, and she would get up immediately and would go off to work on something, as if she had only taken a short nap to get some strength back. And she would say herself that she had only taken a nap, and even scolded us, that we didn't let her have that short period to rest.

But I was still scared and believed Mortutė more, and not what Barborytė said about these episodes, but that time I was scared more than ever. I was so afraid, that my tears overflowed and streamed down my face. The faucets were on full force and I could barely wipe them dry. Something told me that this time was truly the last.

Barborytė and I were very close. She was more important to me than a brother or a sister or any other sort of kid could have been. Even Barborytė used to say the same thing. She used to say that the two of us were the best buddies not only in the whole village, but in the entire parish. Why we were so close — I don't really know, looking back on it. She was old, real old, and me, I wasn't even a teenager. Maybe it was because, as they say, old age and childhood are similar. What they have in common I am not really sure, and I think perhaps those who claim old age and childhood are similar don't really know, either. She was some kind of relative of mine, although even today I can't give our relation a precise name. I doubt that that kind of relation ever really had a one-word name. She was my mother's grandfather's grandmother.[3] No one kept track of and no one knew her age. She herself said at the last Šilinės that she had reached now a round hundred years of age.[4] But my mother and father shook their heads at that. They were certain that Barborytė was intentionally making herself at least a dozen years younger than she really was.

Her life was pretty unique, as she was herself. As she told the story, she was plucked early by a boy, without even having had time to bloom fully. She became sixteen during Šilinės, and she became the bride of Ignatius Matelis, a sole inheritor, just after the potato harvest. He was a rare man: tall, handsome. If he had not been the single inheritor, he probably would have been chosen for the queen's regiment.[5] He didn't even smoke a pipe, and would make no — ahem! — detours while coming back from the market. Even when entertaining guests at home he would only make sure their glasses were filled, but he himself would only touch a glass to his lips for the sake of appearances. And she had been attracted to him, oh yes. Even when a child looking after geese, she couldn't take her eyes off of him. 'If he hadn't hit on me, I would have started running after him,' she used to say. They had lived together so well and easily, as if two fingers stuck to one another. One large, the other small. Only

---

[3] Trans. note: Barborytė was the child's great-great-great grandmother.
[4] Trans. note: Šilinės is a Catholic holy day, the first Sunday in September, associated with the appearance of Mary, the Mother of God, at Šiluva.
[5] Trans. note: Lithuania was occupied by Czarist Russia from the end of the 18th century to 1918. The reference to the queen is to the wife of the czar.

the big one was not fated to enjoy his little one for long. He didn't even have enough time to see all his children grown. He left with one still a babe in arms. But she raised them all and saw them off into the world well. She raised them by herself. If she had wanted she could have married again. She received more than just one single proposal of marriage, and from more than one gallant. But she remained single because she knew that she would never, ever, get another one like that one. Why marry and then, every day, long for the old days and to be sorry you can't bring them back.

Back then, being just a kid, I had no real conception about women's beauty. But I used to hear them say that in her youth Barborytė was very pretty, very lively, and very tiny. She was still lively and tiny even in our buddy days. When I was nine years old, we were the same height. She used to say, 'Buddy, wow, we are completely alike. Me, I'm ninety nine, and you, you are nine, and isn't that the same age, really? And you have caught up to me in height as well. Verutė, take a look, are we the same height?' We would stand together in the middle of the room, back to back, and my mother would take a look to be sure I was not up on my toes, then she'd put a piece of wood across our heads and would confirm that, indeed, we were the same height. Whether Barborytė got up on her toes or not, I don't know even today, because my mother checked us both this way all winter, and we were even every day. But I knew I had to be growing, so I went and asked my mom whether the old woman was growing, too. When I found out that old people can't grow, I became worried that I wouldn't grow any more and that I'd wind up being some sort of munchkin. No one would ever call me anything else. Just 'Hey, there's the Pluikis family munchkin!' I was so worried that I was afraid even to mention it to my mother, but I told Barborytė, when everyone had gone on a Sunday to church, and me & Barborytė had stayed home together. Am I going to stay a munchkin for the rest of my life? Barborytė had laughed at that, and even tears appeared in her eyes, and she clasped me to her bosom. After she regained some composure she said that I am growing, and that I am growing a lot, just that she, when mother measures us, gets up on her toes so that we would still be even and alike, but that she wouldn't be able to do this much any more, because there isn't much higher that she can go, and that she wondered what would happen in the spring when everything begins to bloom and grow, and that before I knew it I would be as high as the treetops at this rate. And that when I grew up to be a man I wouldn't even want to see my old shrunken buddy, so old and wrinkled. I jumped up at once, in tears, to protest that I would never, ever not want to be see or be with her & that even if I were to grow as high as the clouds I'd still be her bestest bestest buddy.

Running down the paths through the fields, those memories ran with me, and my legs tried to go even faster so that Mortutė with her prayers could come over as quick as possible.

Barborytė did not live with us the year-round. She'd go and visit other relatives, who, as she put it, were stretched out helter-skelter over five parishes. She'd leave for a few weeks at a stretch, sometimes even a few months. Those times would be the hardest for me, because there were spaces in them which only Barborytė could have filled. A great fear came over me, that she might leave now and never come back.

When she'd return, she would always say that there was no place as good as our house. Everywhere else she felt as a guest, only; whereas here as soon as she'd step into the house she'd feel really, truly, home. An idea came to me, to ask Mortutė whether, if Barborytė didn't like being in heaven, whether she could come back to her Pluikis family, but I was afraid to. Mortutė was a very serious, bitter woman. Tall, bony, bent forward at the waist, never smiling. At least I'd never seen a smile on her always tightly pressed together lips. She'd even say mean things about Barborytė, but she'd never refuse to attend at a deathbed. Not for Barborytė, but for anyone. Even for those she had already consigned to eternal hellfire. I don't know what she would have said about Barborytė, but I was afraid to ask, anyway. I was afraid that she would say that no one could come back from hell, even if one really didn't like being there.

Maybe she didn't like Barborytė also because Barborytė got along better with my father and not my mother, although it was my mother that she was related to. Mortutė for some reason really didn't like it when Barborytė would say that my father was just like Ignatius. And she called him her son-in-law, and sometimes even Donny-Donatello. I couldn't understand why Mortutė used to get mad at that, and my mother would just laugh, saying that one pea recognizes another, and also that both are just the same sort of incorrigible sinners, and that is why they get on so well together. When I once got up the courage to ask whether my father really was an incorrigible sinner, my mother just said that if everyone was like father, that the earth would be a paradise.

About their being sinners, I could say only this. Neither my father nor Barborytė would go to church every Sunday. My father would often let the horses run free on such days. He used to say that even they have a hard time being tied up in one place all day long. 'Weren't horses created by the same hands which created you? How would you like it if you were kept locked up day and night. During the day to be hitched to a wagon, plough, or suchlike, and in the evening and on holy days in the corral. Such a sight could even anger the good God. And fields and forests are covered by that same sky, so why should they be any worse than tile-roofed churches?'

If my father ever prayed or just spoke straight-out with his God, no one saw or heard. Once, when Mortutė wanted him to take part in her prayers, he said that he only speaks privately with a priest or with God. Looking back, I think now that he prayed just like everyone else, at least sometimes, because I remember seeing him walking about with a rosary in hand. Not within the house nor in the church, but in the fields or in the barnyard.

Barborytė did in truth pray, and she even sang the holy hymns. Everywhere. In the house, in the barnyard, and in the workfields. Even in the forest. She really'd go to the forest quite often, especially when berries and mushrooms and nuts would appear. It used to be so nice to go walk with her in the forest, because she knew her way around very well, and she knew where and when the best berries would be ripe, and where the best mushrooms of every sort, and where the tastiest nuts would be waiting to wind up as a treat for one's palate, as long as one knew how not to drop them into the grass below.

She also knew stories about every bush and tree, why the branches of some types stretch down to the ground, as if looking for something lost, while those of another rise straight into the sky as if they wanted to catch a flying angel by his legs. It was a bit scary, though, when she used to take me there on Sundays, when everyone was at church. Even at High Mass. For that not only Mortutė scolded her, repeatedly, but even my mother. They said that at that time the forest is taken over by all sorts of evil spirits. They would send snakes and swarms of waspts upon those who defy God, or would entice them with pink sparking necklaces hung on the branches of giant knotweed bushes, which, when placed around one's neck, would come alive and choke the wearer to death. Mortutė knew the names of those who had been slain in such a manner or by charmed snakebites, and even the dates of their deaths.

Barborytė did not fear these stories, and she taught me not to pay attention to them. When words of encouragement did not seem to help, she would beat on the greenery with a rosary and holy rope (usually worn by monks) brought back from Siluva, or she would walk around large berry patches while singing some holy hymn so that all of the evil spirits would fly out of that particular, berry-filled, patch. And in truth, while walking with her in the forests, I never saw any snakes, nor any pink gleaming necklaces hung about on branches. Just those who would return from church would find on many Sundays bowls on their main tables, full of blueberries, strawberries, or nuts.

I didn't have to say even one word to Mortutė. When I staggered in, out of breath, across her threshold, she said, 'So it's Barborytė again,' and got up her loom. I only had to confirm her guess.

While she dressed — and she would get dressed up for a deathbed as if she were going to church on Sunday — I had to tell her all of the details. So I did, and as I was telling her, it seemed she was intentionally dragging the time out, so that after so many deathbed attendances she wouldn't have to make a mistake again, that the one attended would not rise after so many (wasted) prayers. I was convinced: if we didn't make it, if we found her dead, no amount of prayers would bring her back.

I wanted to hurry Mortutė up; I wanted to tell her to hurry, but who could tell such a Mortutė anything. I doubt that my mother or father would have had the gumption, and I, a boy barely ten years old, just didn't have enough firepower. She asked, I answered, and she asked me to repeat it all, over and over again, how it happened, how Barborytė slumped down, did she hit her leg very hard into the table. I said I hadn't seen, that no one had seen, and she laced her long black boots, adjusted her skirt, brushed her hair, then put on her black jacket with padded shoulders, then put on a short overcoat with cotton stuffing. When she at last pulled a black, thick shawl from a peg, I was the first at the door. I don't know: maybe she was actually hurrying, maybe all that getting-ready of hers only took a few seconds, but for me it seemed at least a year.

When we went out into the yard, she rather shrewishly asked, 'Do you know why Barborytė always recovers?'

143

Of course I didn't. How could I know such things? But she didn't wait for any answer.

'Because Saint Peter chases her away from the gates. He says, *Go home, reform yourself, throw all the stray winds out of your head, live according to God's law for a while, and then I'll let you in.* But eventually she'll run out of chances: even Saint Peter will run out of patience, and he'll throw her down you-know-where.'

Mortutė didn't specify to where Barborytė was to be thrown, and immediately began the Litany for the Dying. She was so loud that echoes came back from the village buildings, and she ordered me to say the second-parts. While we were near buildings I answered in a whisper, even though Mortutė would glare at me angrily. But when we were in the fields, then I really opened up my throat.

'All ye holy apostles and evangelists, pray for her. All ye holy disciples of the Lord, pray for her. All ye holy innocents, pray for her...' sounded out over the fields. I don't know what Mortutė was aiming for, but me, I was shouting as loud as I could so that all the saints would hear and would let Barborytė get back up, just the same as always, just the same as when she said the woodpecker had brought the wagtail and the half-day. In my life, I have prayed many times thereafter, but never as fervently and devoutly.

When we entered the house, Barborytė had recovered consciousness, but was very weak. She looked at the ceiling, and then turned her eyes upon me and smiled. For me this was a sign that the saints had heard my voice and had restored Barborytė. But Mortutė thought otherwise. She came up, fixed Barborytė's hair, sprinkled her with holy water, and said,

'So Saint Peter still doesn't want to open heaven's gates? But we'll ask him nicely, maybe he'll take pity on you, if you aren't carrying anything with you, hidden away. And my oh my, if you had only heard little Mike, how he prayed, even the fields echoed with his words. His prayer alone might have caused Saint Peter to feel for you, Barborytė.'

Only my mother was in the house. Father had ridden out to get the priest. My brother and sisters were running to the neighbors to give them the news, that a priest has been gone-for. Even if all alone, my mother had been able to cover the beds with new coverings, the table with a white tablecloth, and the clay floor sparkled with newly sprinkled yellow sand. Mortutė lost no time either. Having spoken with the patient, she looked the house over so that my mother would not have forgotten anything, and at once said that there was no cross on the table. While my mother was wiping and shining one which she had taken from the windowsill, Mortutė turned and again bent down over to the sufferer.

'While they are coming with the priest, you do some hard thinking. Not only about the present, but about your youth as well, so that, God forbid, you wouldn't have been holding out. You can hide things from people, but not from God. And do you want little Mike to hold the candle like the last time?'

The first time Barborytė had taken to what we thought was her deathbed; they had chased us kids out of the house. They had said it was not good for children to see a person die: they might even catch something. Then she had regained consciousness and had asked where Mikey was. Learning that Mikey had been made to go outside, she demanded he be called in at once, and she had remonstrated to everyone, especially to Mortutė, that at the hour of her death that everyone had separated her from her bestest buddy.

'Mikey,' she had said then, 'Next time don't listen to them. Stay with me to the end. When you are beside me, even dying will be easier for me. And hold the grief-candle. With you shining that light, it will be easier for me to find my way through the forlorn darkness.'

For such talk Mortutė had scolded her, called her a pagan, and had even threatened to tell the prelate.[6] But she let me stay in the room, and even let me hold the candle which Barborytė called the 'grief-candle.'

But this time Barborytė did not reply to Mortutė. She just stared unblinkingly straight up at the ceiling. She didn't blink even when Mortutė waved her hand right by Barborytė's eyes.

'Oh Jesus! Her eyes are going glassy, looking up, and we are just standing around and allowing the evil spirits to grab her soul. Where is the holy water? Where is the candle?!'

My mother had everything ready. She gave me the candle and lit a match. With a shaking hand she tried to light the wick which was bent to one side, while Mortutė splashed the windows, doors, and every corner of the house with holy water, even getting up on a stool to splash the top of the high stove, where, they say, devils like to warm themselves and to watch what the people in the house are up to.

Having sprinkled everything, she drew her chair into the middle of the room, took up her prayerbook, and sat down so she could comfortably see the patient. As Mortutė was getting herself situated, it seems to me that at one point Barborytė winked at me with the corner of her eye, just like she used to do when she wanted only the two of us to know something. If Mortutė had looked at her prayerbook, maybe Barborytė would have given me another wink. But Mortutė never opened the book; she just held it, perhaps like a holy object. Because she knew all the prayers by heart, her eyes never left the patient.

---

[6] Trans. note: Apparently what sets Mortutė off is that Barborytė supposes that she will not be long in purgatory.

146

'Acts of virtues, necessary for salvation. Act of faith. My God, because you are the first and perfect truth, I believe strongly in everything which you have revealed to the Catholic church and which that church has taught me to believe... Mikey, hold the candle straight. You are dripping wax on the bed! ... I believe there in only one God in three Persons, and these Persons are ... Mikey, watch what you are doing! You are dripping the wax again. Say the act of faith together with me... The Father, the Son, and the Holy Spirit. I believe that Jesus was made flesh by the Holy Spirit of the Virgin Mary ... Louder, Mikey. Like when you prayed the litany of the dying. Open up your mouth. Don't you want Saint Peter to open up those gates for Barborytė?'

I wanted that, oh yes, I did, but I wanted even more that Barborytė would get up again, like she did the last time and the times before that. But Barborytė herself confused me a bit. While Mortutė gave me grief, Barborytė gave me an ever-so-slight smile. Only for me, and for no one else. And when Mortutė told me to open up my mouth, she winked at me again with her left eye, and I barely kept from letting out a laugh. My restraining myself was aided by the fact that more people were arriving to wait for the priest. The men were staying in the yard to chat and to share pipe tobacco, and the women came in, one by one, into the room, finding room for themselves and joining in with Mortutė's prayers. Having recited the litanies of faith, hope, love and mercy, Mortutė got up, came up to Barborytė, looked at her face, bending down put her ear to Barborytė's mouth to hear whether she was still breathing, and turning to everyone gathered there said in a whisper,

'She's getting ready. We'll recite the litany of the dying. She'll probably not hang on long enough to receive the Holy Sacrament.'

'Easter is not long past. What could she do during those few days,' my mother interjected, but Mortutė wiped it away as if with the back of her hand.

147

'The Good God will understand, not us. If she doesn't hang on, the priest will know what to do. It is not our place to give advice. While we have time, let us pray, let's ask that God be merciful.'

And not pausing to allow any neighbor woman to say anything, Mortutė began.

'I love you, my God, with my whole heart, with my whole soul, with my whole being... Barborytė, if you can hear my words, repeat them with me, with all of us. If you can't say them out loud, say them in your mind. God can hear it either way... And I love you more and more because of yourself alone...'

I tried to repeat after Mortutė myself, but all sorts of memories got in the way. They ran and ran through my head, the places Barborytė and I had been together, what we had seen, what we had said, how last fall we found whole bunch of red-pine mushrooms, how returning home I slipped along the bank into the creek and got completely wet, up to my chin, and lost all of my red-pine mushrooms, and how afterwards both of us had gathered them from the creek and had were soaked, both of us, when we got home. The day had been very fair, but Barborytė told everyone there had been a sudden shower on the other side of the forest and had soaked the both of us. I looked at Barborytė's face and thought, could such a lie keep the gates of heaven shut against her?

'The candle, Mikey, the candle! You are dozing off again? If it weren't for the dying-one's request, I would have taken that candle from you myself.'

When Morta spoke, it would often make one start. And that's what happened then. I started so hard that I nearly dropped the candle. I was sure she was going to jump up and tear it out of my hand. I looked around to see where my mother was, for some support, although I really didn't expect to receive any. During a deathbed attendance, Mortutė was in charge and no one else. But this time she didn't jump up or take the candle from me. Perhaps because she had reached the end of the prayer. So having scolded me, she continued without a pause,

'... and may the everlasting light shine upon me. Jesus, Jesus, Jesus, whom I love heartfully. Jesus be my Jesus. Jesus, Mary, and holy Joseph, I give up my soul to you!'

I was reciting those words along with everyone, but when she got to those last words, Mortutė shouted them so loudly that chills went up and down my spine and I could no longer hold back my tears. I didn't see my mother come and put one arm around me and take the candle with the other. But I didn't let it go, either, and we both held it together for a time, and then she said,

'Let's go into the other room. I'll get you something to eat. You haven't eaten anything since the morning.'

I just shook my head. I still couldn't say anything: I was still fighting back tears. They were running down my mother's face, too. Only Mortutė was immovable. She was still going on with another litany in the same tone, with the same grim expression on her face. The litany for the dying, the same one we had spoken and shouted out in the village and in the fields. This time I did not join in. My mother didn't, either. Both of us stayed there, together, she with her arm around me, and both of us held up that candle. This was not the first time we were attending at this deathbed, but then I hadn't felt as bad as this.

It seemed to me that something very big and strong was coming, and when it got here here it would swoop Barborytė up in its big hand, and that would be that, I'd never see her again.

I heard the litany go on. I heard the even tones of Mortutė's voice. I heard the answers of the women, which even back then I had already learned by heart. But I felt as if I were in a dream. But when she got to the part which went, 'Go forth, Christian soul, from this world, in the Name of God the Father Almighty, Who created you; in the Name of Jesus Christ, Son of the Living God, Who suffered for you; in the Name of the Holy Ghost, Who was poured forth upon you,' I wanted to scream, 'No! No! No!!' but I couldn't. A strange feeling came over me and I couldn't move. A fear I'd never felt before, that I'd never see Barborytė again, that I'd never hear the cheerful sound of her voice again. I think the same feeling came over my mother, because I felt how she gripped me even harder, as if Morta and her chorus of women were trying to send *me* from this world, too. It was a while until I found that I was squeezing the candle so tightly that the wax was melting in my hot grip.

I started to recover when the women finished the 'Litany of the Blessed Virgin' and all of them softly began to intone, 'Jesus, Jesus, Jesus ...' After several repetitions of this, Barborytė sighed loudly and turned to the wall. Mortutė got up from her chair, turned to the women and whispered,

'She is dying. Now she is really dying. Let us pray, but quietly, queitly; let her soul calmly depart from this world.'

She began to intone, in a whisper, 'Jesus, Jesus, Jesus ...' and the women joined in. 'Jesus, Jesus.' The little house was filled with this rythmic whispering, such an eerie rythmic music, which was at the same time a type of chills-down-your-back lullabye.

But suddenly in the middle of this rythmic whispering, we heard a soft giggling. Mortutė jumped up from her chair and across to the bed.

'Barborytė, are you giggling?'

'Yes it's me, dearie, who else?'

'Oh my, I thought it was the evil one laughing at us, snatching your soul right from under our noses!'

'What would he want with my little old, dried-up soul? He gets enough big & fat ones,' she said in a perfectly clear voice. Then she started to giggle again.

'So what are you laughing about? Maybe at how the evil spirits are being chased away from you by God's angels?'

'No, dearie. How could I see such things with my sinful eyes? No. I was remembering my first time.'

Mortutė grabbed her own head with her hands.

'What, you… Have you completely lost your mind? Here we are, praying, paving the way for her to heaven with holy prayers, and what is she doing?!! Don't you even fear God anymore?? She can't get by without disgusting stuff!! You don't need prayers: you need a whip to be taken to you!!'

Barborytė turned away from the wall and sat up. This movement was totally coordinated and quick, as if she hadn't been at death's door.

'Mortutė, Mortutė, why are you always so hard, like a dried-out splinter of wood. Isn't the first time blessed by God himself, so why do you jump and say 'disgusting, disgusting.' If it were disgusting, God would not have blessed it. And if laughter comes over someone, what of it? Isn't laughter from that same God? You know, I was such a stupid little thing back then, barely out of childhood. Who knows, maybe even Lord God smiled at my naiveté, because Ignatius, well, he laughed! Oh, back then I was embarrased, but later both of us would laugh, remembering.'

And she started giggling again, and then began to laugh out loud.

'Oh, if I were to tell you the whole story … if I were to tell you …' she said, in between bursts of laughter. 'But I will tell you, sometime. When I am stronger, I'll tell you, I'll tell the story to everyone. And you too, Mortutė, you'll laugh, too. You'll see.'

Then she laughed with gusto again, and then the laughter turned to giggles, and, as if held up by an invisible hand, Barborytė fell back softly on the pillows. And then her eyes became a bit strange, then moved up towards her forehead, as if she were trying to see something standing at the head of her bed.

For a while there was total silence in the house. Then Mortutė got up from her chair and went slowly up to the bed. She stood there a long time, then nodded her head several times and turned towards all of us who were there. She remained silent a long time. Maybe she was thinking of what to do, what to say, or maybe she couldn't figure out what to make of her own thoughts.

'What can we do, when she herself has chosen her own destination,' she pronounced her sentence at last.

The other women were also dismayed and discomfited. They shot glances at one another and had no idea what to say or do.

'What can we do? Why, *pray!*' interjected Mrs. Abraitis, who herself probably wasn't very far in years from Barborytė. 'We can do what we came here to do. And you, Mortutė, *judge not, lest thou be judged!* Perhaps God is waiting for her there with open arms. Let's show some humility.'

She opened up a book and began,

'Stay you saints of God, come you heavenly Angels, Virtues, Thrones and Powers, receive this soul, and may He award her a place among those who stand before Him for ever...'

My mother let go of me and stood up and shut Barborytė's eyes.

That is when I could hold it no longer. I began to cry out loud and then jumped up and ran out. Out through the praying women, through the men in the forecourt smoking their pipes, through the orchard, and into the barn's furthest corner. For the first time in my life all I wanted was to be alone. Totally alone.

* * *

Jurgis Jankus was born in Lithuania in 1906. He already enjoyed an excellent reputation as a novelist in pre-war Lithuania when he had to flee his homeland to escape the Soviet occupation. Settling in Rochester, New York, he worked in factories and raised four boys with his wife, Kotryna. He wrote at night and on the weekends, and published a number of collections of short stories and two plays. In 1991 he traveled to Lithuania, which had newly re-established its independence, for the first time since WWII. There he greatly enjoyed the many literary events which were organized in his honor. Jurgis Jankus died in 2002 and is buried in Rochester, New York.

This short story was originally published in a collection of Jurgis Jankus' short stories entitled *Tėvas Venancijus ir jo Matilda* (Lietuviškas knygų klubas 1988). This English translation was translated especially for this present collection and has never before been published.

ABOUT THE EDITOR AND TRANSLATOR

Tadas Klimas is an attorney and associate professor of law.

By decree of the President of Lithuania, Tadas Klimas in 2009 was granted the title of Cavalier of the Knight's Cross of the Lithuanian Order of Merit.

That high honor joins the National Intelligence Medal of Achievement; one of the highest medals of the United States, bestowed upon him in 1992 by the DCI (Director, Central Intelligence) Robert Gates. Dr. Gates at the time of this writing is the U.S. Secretary of Defense.

Klimas, a former Special Agent of the Federal Bureau of Investigation, has been dean of a law school, chief legal counsel to the Speaker of the Lithuanian parliament, and has taught law in the United States, Lithuania, Spain, Brazil, & Vietnam. He is the author of several books, among them the law school casebook and treatise, *Comparative Contract Law* (Carolina Academic Press 2006). Tadas Klimas can be reached at tadasklimas@yahoo.com or tk@ltlaw.lt.